The Big Book of
Knights, Nobles & Knaves

Adaptation and abridgment by Alissa Heyman
Original Spanish text adapted by Francesc Miralles Contijoch
Illustrations by Adrià Fruitós

Library of Congress Cataloging-in-Publication Data Available

STERLING and the distinctive Sterling logo are registered trademarks of Sterling Publishing Co., Inc.

10 9 8 7 6 5 4 3 2 1

Published in 2008 by Sterling Publishing Co., Inc.
387 Park Avenue South, New York, NY 10016

Published by Parramón Ediciones, S.A., Barcelona, Spain.
Originally published in Spain under the title
El Gran Libro de Las Leyendas Medievales

Distributed in Canada by Sterling Publishing
℅ Canadian Manda Group, 165 Dufferin Street
Toronto, Ontario, Canada M6K 3H6
Distributed in the United Kingdom
by GMC Distribution Services, Castle Place, 166 High Street,
Lewes, East Sussex, England BN7 1XU
Distributed in Australia by Capricorn Link (Australia) Pty. Ltd.
P.O. Box 704, Windsor, NSW 2756, Australia

Printed in China

Sterling ISBN 978-1-4027-6241-3

For information about custom editions, special sales, premium and corporate purchases, please contact Sterling Special Sales Department at 800-805-5489 or specialsales@sterlingpublishing.com

The Big Book of Knights, Nobles & Knaves

Illustrated by
Adrià Fruitós

Abridged and Adapted by
Alissa Heyman

STERLING

New York / London
www.sterlingpublishing.com/kids

Contents

Introduction

The exhilarating legends of the Middle Ages present magical and historic lands inhabited by fire-breathing dragons, clever wizards, valiant kings, gallant knights, treacherous knaves, kidnapped queens, maidens trapped in towers, merry bandits, terrifying beasts, and more.

Though many centuries lie between the modern world and the Middle Ages, medieval legends continue to excite the imagination and act as a constant inspiration for contemporary stories.

In the Middle Ages very few people knew how to read; most were illiterate. The few books that existed were copied by hand, since the printing press had not yet been invented. Instead of through the written word, tales were spread orally—that is, by word of mouth, and no one knew who their original authors might be. The person who played a leading role in spreading these stories far and wide was called the minstrel. The minstrel was a professional entertainer, a poet and singer who traveled from town to town with a harp or lute (a kind of antique guitar). He sang ballads and recited poems that he had learned by heart about noble heroes and terrifying villains.

But at times, people who knew how to read and write—mostly members of the educated clergy—would document the stories in writing so that they could be handed down through time. And so there were written records of the poems that told of the exploits of a hero or of a whole people. These epic poems were known by the French phrase "chansons de geste" or "songs of deeds."

Each country had its favorite "chanson de geste." *The Song of Roland* or *La Chanson de Roland*, based very loosely on a historical event—the defeat suffered by the rearguard of Emperor Charlemagne's army at Roncesvalles—was the favorite of the French.

In Spain, the most famous was *The Song of My Cid* or the *Cantar del Mío Cid*, inspired by the last years in the life of the Castilian knight Rodrigo Díaz de Vivar, unjustly banished from his city. *The Song of the Nibelungs* or *The Nibelungenlied*, a magical and tragic tale about the Germanic tribes, was told over and over in Germany.

In England, Arthurian romances were extremely popular. They recounted the many adventures of King Arthur and his Knights of the Round Table who lived in Camelot. These tales concerned courtly love, chivalry, quests for honor in battle, and the search for the Holy Grail. Arthurian legends traveled across Europe, and poets such as France's Chrétien de Troyes and Germany's Wolfram von Eschenbach wrote their own versions of the tales, which have been preserved in manuscripts down through the centuries.

Also in England, there existed many popular legends about the beloved outlaw, Robin Hood, who stole from the rich and gave to the poor, as well as the tragic love stories of *Tristan and Isolde* and *Romeo and Juliet*, which both chronicle the lives of ill-fated young lovers.

Imagine you are in the square of a little town. Suddenly a ripple of excitement runs through the crowd. "The minstrel is here!" a woman shouts. The adults drop the work they are doing. The children hurry to meet the new arrival who wears a cape and a broad-brimmed hat. He sits down against the trunk of a tree and, surrounded by an eager crowd, he plucks the first notes on his lute and begins to tell his rousing tale . . .

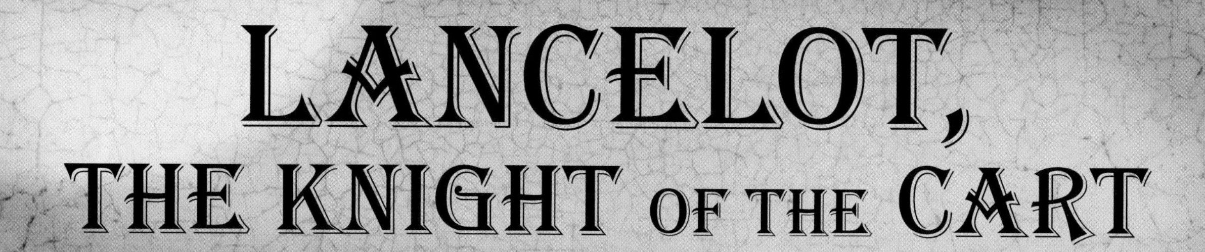

LANCELOT, THE KNIGHT OF THE CART

Origin of the Legend

Sir Lancelot is one of the most famous knights of King Arthur's Round Table. There are many medieval legends about Lancelot and he is most often portrayed as a noble knight, worthy of great respect, who plays an important role in many of King Arthur's victories. However, Lancelot's love for the king's wife, Queen Guinevere, causes great conflict among the Round Table knights, and helps lead to the downfall of Arthur's reign, as Lancelot is divided between loyalty to his king and his love for Guinevere.

Chrétien de Troyes, a renowned French court poet, who has been called by some the inventor of the modern novel, wrote **Lancelot, the Knight of the Cart** in the late twelfth century. The poem was one of five Arthurian romances written by Chrétien. In it Lancelot represents the ideals of chivalry—he exhibits bravery, mercy, and compassion.

Chrétien was the first known author to write about the love between Lancelot and Guinevere, as well as the first to write about the Holy Grail.

The Kidnapping of Queen Guinevere

One day, when King Arthur had gathered the lords and ladies of the court of Camelot together for a celebration, an unknown knight presented himself and challenged the king.

"I have made the knights and maidens of your land my captives," the stranger declared. "If you wish to have them returned, find a knight who deserves all your confidence and send him, along with Queen Guinevere, into the woods. There we will fight. If the knight defeats me, he may bring the queen back and I will free all the prisoners."

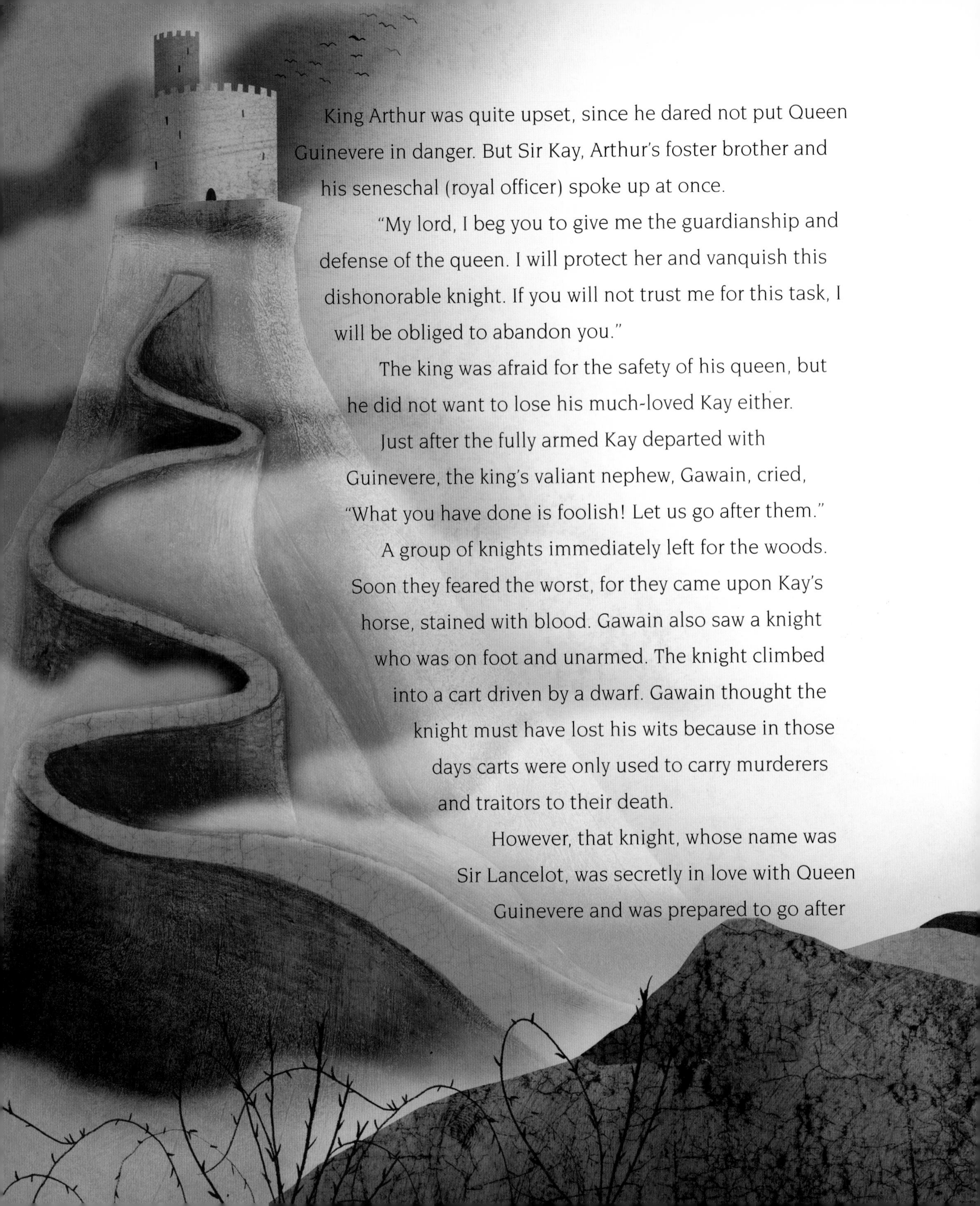

King Arthur was quite upset, since he dared not put Queen Guinevere in danger. But Sir Kay, Arthur's foster brother and his seneschal (royal officer) spoke up at once.

"My lord, I beg you to give me the guardianship and defense of the queen. I will protect her and vanquish this dishonorable knight. If you will not trust me for this task, I will be obliged to abandon you."

The king was afraid for the safety of his queen, but he did not want to lose his much-loved Kay either.

Just after the fully armed Kay departed with Guinevere, the king's valiant nephew, Gawain, cried, "What you have done is foolish! Let us go after them."

A group of knights immediately left for the woods. Soon they feared the worst, for they came upon Kay's horse, stained with blood. Gawain also saw a knight who was on foot and unarmed. The knight climbed into a cart driven by a dwarf. Gawain thought the knight must have lost his wits because in those days carts were only used to carry murderers and traitors to their death.

However, that knight, whose name was Sir Lancelot, was secretly in love with Queen Guinevere and was prepared to go after her, even if he had to disgrace himself by riding in the hangman's cart. He had just lost his horse in a fight, so he had no mount to ride, and he knew he would rather be dishonored for riding in the cart than for failing to rescue the lady he loved.

After that, in each town he passed through, people scorned and ridiculed him, tauntingly calling him the Knight of the Cart.

To the Kingdom of No Return

Undaunted in his search, Lancelot continued on. Along the way he met a maid and begged her to tell him—if she knew—who the man was who had kidnapped Queen Guinevere and where he lived.

"Prince Meleagant, a strong and terrible knight," the girl replied, "has taken her to the kingdom from which no foreigner returns. You can only enter it with the permission of King Bagdemagu, Meleagant's father, and the only way in is across two perilous bridges. One is an underwater bridge. It is submerged and all men who try to cross it drown. The other is the Sword Bridge, made from the narrow, sharp blade of a sword."

"Say no more, for I have no time to waste."

And with that, Lancelot continued determinedly on his way.

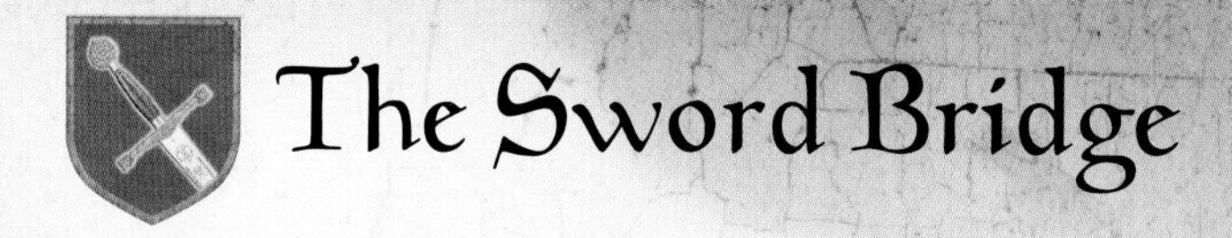

The Sword Bridge

Many were the dangers that Lancelot had to confront before reaching the bridges that protected the castle where Meleagant made his home, but he was able to overcome all of them because of his love for Guinevere.

Finally, he found himself before the sunken bridge. The water covering the bridge was so black, thick, and churning, it was as frightening as if it was the devil's stream. The raging water seemed bottomless, yet Lancelot was able to cross unharmed.

The Sword Bridge, made out of a sturdy sword the length of two lances, was held up by only a tree trunk at each end and seemed about to topple and fall.

When two knights saw that Lancelot seemed about to cross it they hurried to stop him.

"Don't do it, foolish man. You will not be able to cross—the sword's blade will wound you terribly, and besides, it will not be able to hold your weight. But even if you succeed in crossing it will do no good. Do you not see those fierce lions that await you on the other side?"

"Gentlemen, I thank you for your advice, but I would rather die than turn back."

This said, Lancelot accomplished a great feat: he crossed the Sword Bridge by crawling on his hands and knees despite the pain and agony. And though he reached the other side covered with terrible wounds, he was still alive. Once there he found that the terrifying lions had vanished, as they were nothing but the work of a magic spell.

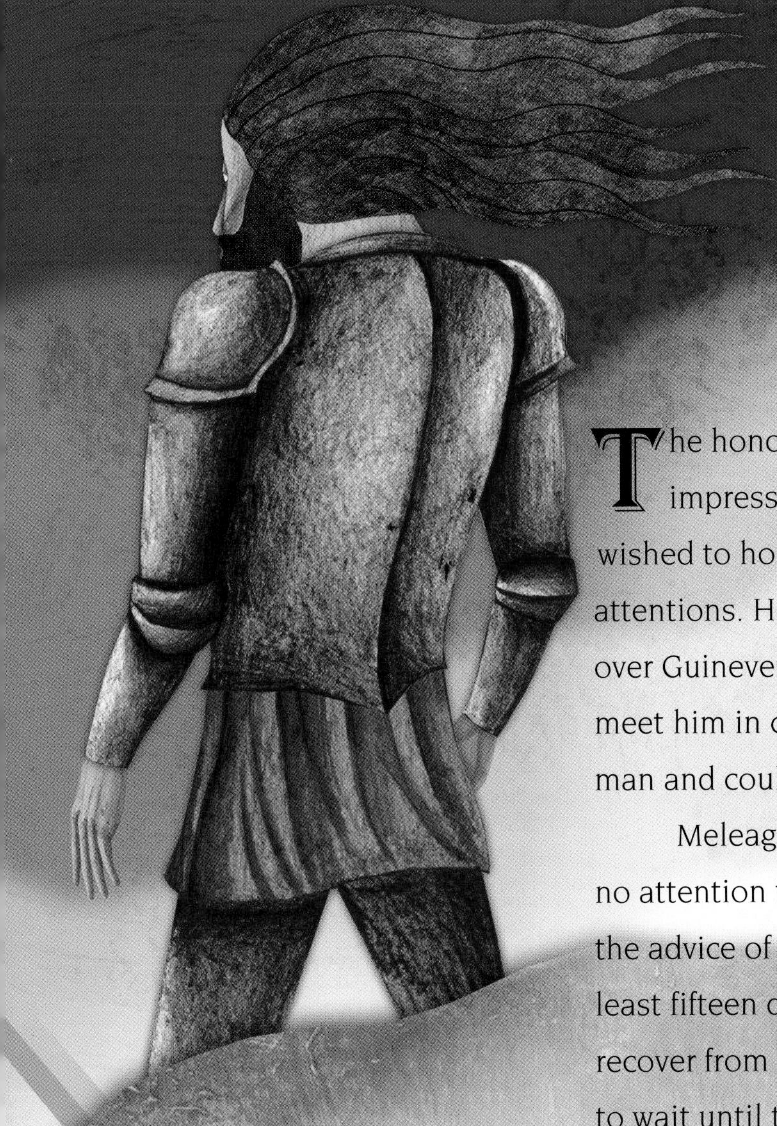

The Great Combat

The honorable King Bagdemagu was so impressed by such a heroic deed that he wished to honor Lancelot with all sorts of attentions. He advised his son, Meleagant, to hand over Guinevere to Lancelot voluntarily and not to meet him in combat, since he was too powerful a man and could not be beaten.

Meleagant was stubborn, however, and paid no attention to his father. Nor did Lancelot follow the advice of the king, who wished him to rest at least fifteen days before fighting so that he might recover from his wounds. Lancelot would only agree to wait until the next day.

On the morning of the combat a great crowd gathered before the castle tower. The king kept trying to make peace between the two knights until the last minute, but it was useless.

The two mounted competitors rode at each other and struck their lances with such force that both shivered and broke into fragments. They then drew their swords and fought on foot. For a moment Lancelot had the worst of it, since the many cuts in his hands prevented him from wielding his sword with all of his might.

However, a wise maiden who was with Guinevere and knew that he drew all his strength from love of the queen, cried out to him. "Lancelot, look who is here and who cannot take her eyes off of you."

On seeing the queen, Lancelot mustered all his strength and was able to gain the advantage to such a point that Meleagant looked upon the verge of death.

King Bagdemagu turned to implore Guinevere. "My lady, I have not for one moment ceased to care for you while you have been a captive here through my son's folly. Return the favor to me and beg Lancelot for the life of him who, though perhaps unworthy to live, is still my son."

Lancelot and Meleagant heard these words and ceased to fight. But Meleagant was so dishonest and stubborn that he claimed to have won, though everyone knew he was lying. At last they made peace when they agreed that Meleagant would surrender the queen to Lancelot on the condition that one year from this day the two men would meet in combat again, this time in Camelot. If Meleagant then succeeded in beating Lancelot, the queen would return to King Bagdemagu's kingdom with Meleagant, and no one at Arthur's court would hold her back.

The Final Combat

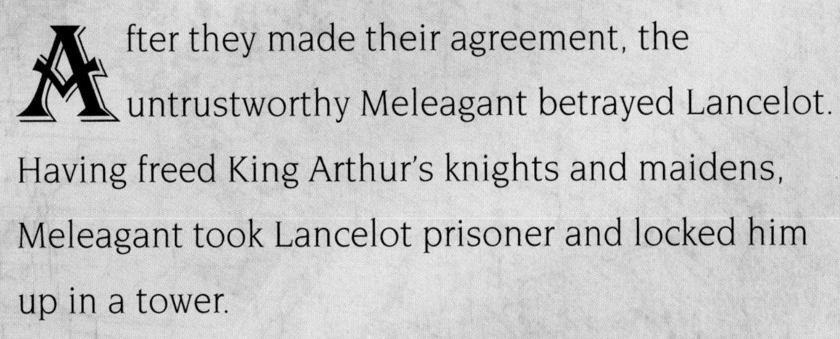

After they made their agreement, the untrustworthy Meleagant betrayed Lancelot. Having freed King Arthur's knights and maidens, Meleagant took Lancelot prisoner and locked him up in a tower.

When the day of the final combat arrived, Meleagant appeared at King Arthur's castle, not expecting to find his opponent there. He had no idea that Lancelot had managed to escape.

Everyone at the court showed great joy on seeing Lancelot arrive. Queen Guinevere, who secretly returned Lancelot's love, did not even wish to be present at the fight, since she was afraid everyone would be able to see the love in her eyes.

The two men prepared to fight to the death. Lancelot was so angry at the treachery he had suffered that he did not take long to deal his opponent a fatal wound. And no one at King Arthur's Court mourned Meleagant's death, since all knew that his heart held nothing but foul intentions.

That night there was a great feast in the castle. Guinevere and Lancelot did not dare dance together. But they were able to gaze lovingly at one another from a distance, both deeply moved by the other's devotion.

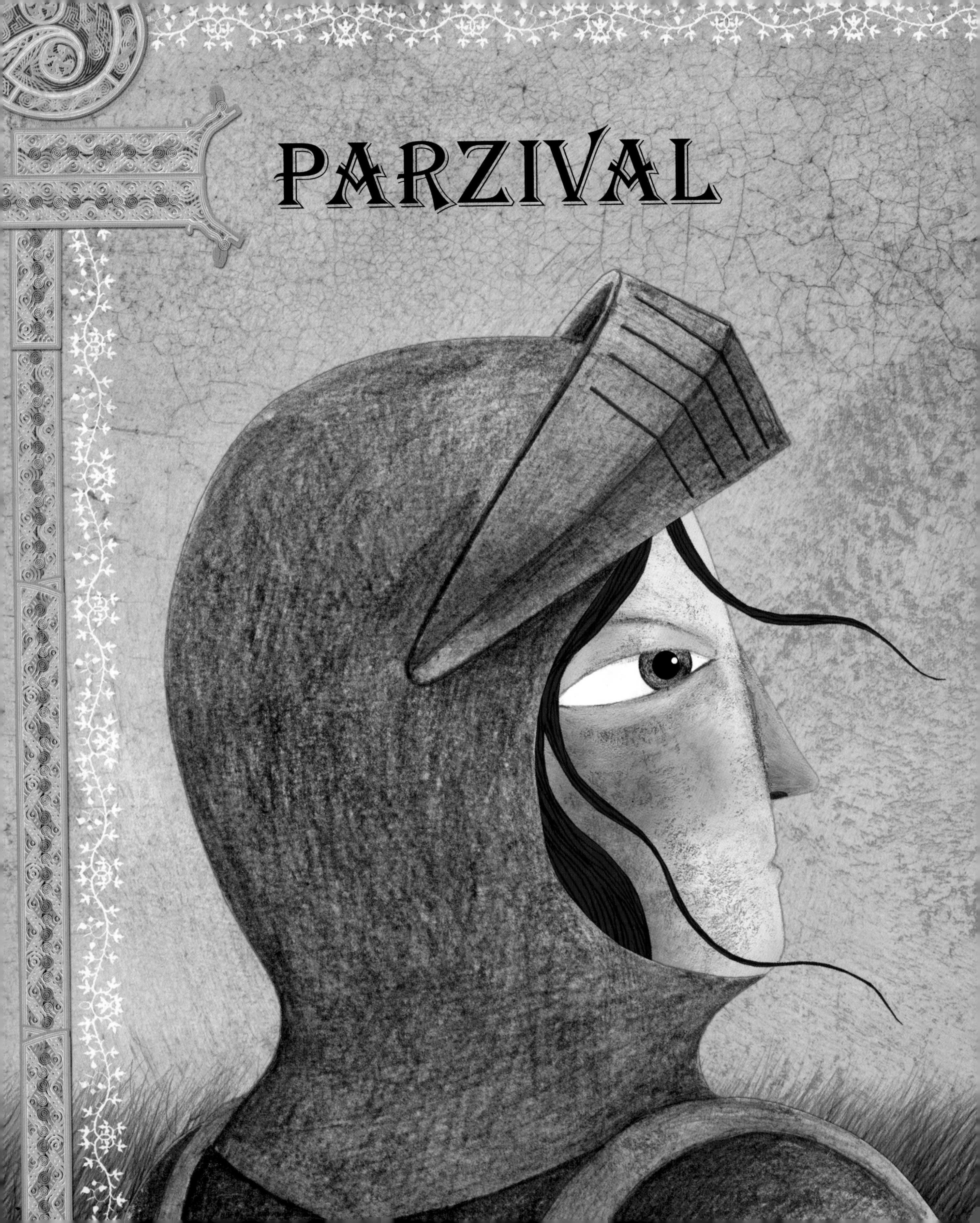
PARZIVAL

Origin of the Legend

Parzival is a major medieval German epic poem written by the knight and poet Wolfram von Eschenbach in the early thirteenth century. Eschenbach took the French poet Chrétien de Troyes's *Perceval, the Story of the Grail*, written in the late twelfth century, as the inspiration for writing his own version of the legend. Chrétien was the first to link the subject of the Holy Grail to the knight Parzival; however, he died before he could finish the poem. Eschenbach was the first to write about the Grail in German. The theme of the Grail was taken up by other medieval authors and has always remained mysterious in part because of the many different versions of the legend.

Eschenbach's *Parzival* recounts the many adventures of the hero (also known as Perceval or Parsifal) as he journeys from an innocent youth, ignorant in the ways of the world, to become a more experienced man knowledgeable in the arts of chivalry and knighthood. The story focuses on Parzival's lengthy quest for the Holy Grail. It can be seen as a coming-of-age tale.

In 1882, the renowned opera composer Richard Wagner based his famous final opera, *Parsifal*, on the epic story, and so it has survived through the centuries to be enjoyed by modern audiences.

Innocent Youth

In the deepest part of a secluded forest in Wales, a young man named Parzival had been brought up in complete ignorance of the world by his mother. After her husband, a king and knight, was killed in battle, the grief-stricken queen had sworn she would raise her son in ignorance of the ways of knighthood and chivalry. In order to protect him from the fate that had befallen her husband, she did not tell him of his noble origins.

But as chance would have it, Parzival, out wandering in the woods one day, came upon a group of King Arthur's knights dressed all in gold and silver. They wore shining armor and dazzling helmets, and they carried shields and powerful lances.

The inexperienced boy, who had never seen anything like these impressive knights, was so awed that he fell to his knees before them, taking them for angels.

"Boy, have no fear," one of them said to him.

"Are you an angel?"

"By my faith, I am only a knight."

"And what is a knight?"

The men were amazed at the naïveté of the young man. They explained to him what a shield was and what armor was for, and they also told him that there was a court where King Arthur made knights of men who were worthy of such honor.

By the time he said goodbye to that magnificent group of knights, Parzival had already decided what his destiny would be. The next morning he set out for King Arthur's court, though not before saying farewell to his heartbroken mother, who dressed her son in fool's rags in hopes that he would not be taken seriously by the knights.

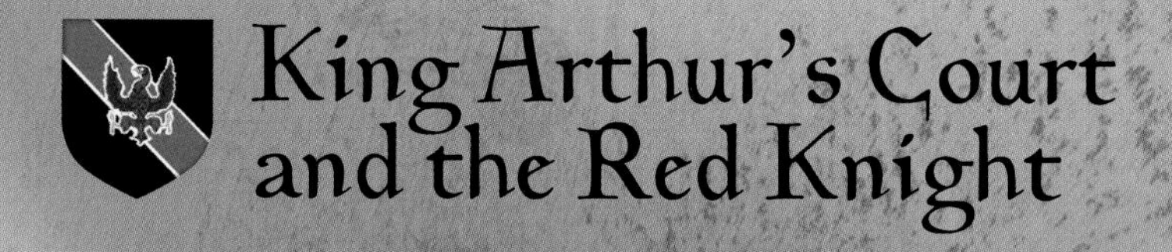

King Arthur's Court and the Red Knight

Parzival rode until he came to King Arthur's court. He saw a knight leaving the castle wearing red armor and bearing beautiful weapons of the same color. In his hand, the knight held a golden goblet. Parzival decided he would ask the king for armor just like that.

On entering the court he found the king very upset by the visit of the Red Knight, who had come to challenge Arthur's right to some of his lands.

Parzival asked the king to make him a knight and give him the Red Knight's armor. He seemed so childish asking such a foolish request that Sir Kay laughed and told him to go get the armor himself. As Parzival was leaving to do so, a maiden smiled at him.

"One day there will be no better knight than you," she predicted.

Sir Kay became so angry that he slapped the girl. Parzival vowed that he would punish Kay for that some day, but at that moment he hastened to leave the court to go in search of the Red Knight.

When he caught up with the Red Knight, Parzival called out for him to surrender his arms. Surprised at a challenge from a boy who was not even wearing armor, the knight lifted his lance and struck Parzival on the back, thinking that would be enough to discourage him. But Parzival dealt him a deadly blow with his javelin.

Parzival then asked one of King Arthur's knights to take the Red Knight's goblet back to court and to tell the maiden whom Kay had struck that he would return one day to avenge her. He took the Red Knight's armor and weapons and rode off.

Grail Castle

Continuing on, Parzival met a wise older knight, Gornemant, who became Parzival's mentor, teaching him the noble arts of chivalry and fighting. Parzival was quick to learn, but had trouble behaving like a knight. Thus Gornemant counseled him to keep silent in order to avoid asking naïve questions.

Having learned how to use the weapons of a knight, Parzival continued his journey and soon found himself before a great castle. The lord of the castle, King Anfortas, welcomed him, but could not do so standing up because he was injured and unable to move on his own.

Parzival was feasted with a banquet fit for a king. What most surprised him was that, several times during the meal, a procession of maids and knights passed by.

Among them was a page carrying a lance from whose point drops of blood continually dripped. He also saw a beautiful maiden who carried in her hands a grail, or chalice, that shone so brightly that even fire seemed pale beside its other-worldly glow.

Parzival was burning with curiosity to find out why the lance bled and who was served with this Grail, as well as to ask Anfortas how he became injured, but he remembered Gornemant's advice, and asked no questions at all.

The next morning Parzival found the castle entirely empty. Had the events of the night before been just an illusion?

Meeting Gawain

Meanwhile, news of Parzival's remarkable exploits was continually coming to King Arthur's court. One day, when the king learned that Parzival had beaten one of the most famous and feared knights of the land, whom everyone thought was invincible, Arthur decided to go out with his entourage and find Parzival.

They traveled far, journeying across snow-covered mountains. Many days later, one of the king's knights caught a glimpse of a young man who seemed to be lost in thought. He went to give the king the news, and Arthur ordered that the young man be brought to him. Sir Kay offered to do this for the king.

Kay approached the young man and spoke roughly. "Vassal," he snarled, "you will come before the king or I'll make you pay dearly for it."

Sir Kay hadn't recognized that the youth was none other than Parzival himself. Parzival, seeing himself treated so rudely, dealt Sir Kay such a blow with his lance that he knocked Kay off his horse and broke his arm.

Kay returned injured to the court where Sir Gawain, King Arthur's nephew, swore to bring back the boy. The virtues of the chivalrous Gawain were famous throughout the kingdom. When he reached Parzival and introduced himself graciously, Parzival was glad to meet him, since he had heard such extraordinary things about him.

Gawain asked that he go with him to King Arthur's court, telling Parzival that the man he had just defeated was none other than Sir Kay.

Seeing that his vengeance had been taken, Parzival went with Gawain, and at the court everyone was very pleased to finally meet the young man about whom they had heard so many extraordinary tales. King Arthur held a great feast in his honor.

The Prophecy

One day at the court, Parzival spied a woman riding on a mule. The woman was ugly and deformed, and he thought she must be a witch. In fact, her name was Cundrie and she was a messenger of the grail.

"Oh, Parzival," she said to him, "wretched are you, since you did not take fortune when you found it! You entered the house of the Lord Anfortas, the Fisher King—for that is what the king of the Holy Grail is called—and you saw the lance that bleeds, yet did not dare ask why. Nor did you wish to know who was served with the glowing Grail. If you had asked these questions, you would have broken the terrible spell on that man who is so ill. The injured king would have healed and his barren lands would have flourished. But now evil things will continue to happen, and it is all your fault."

On hearing the woman's words, Parzival felt terrible sadness and shame at having lost his honor. He immediately swore before King Arthur that he would not rest until he had found the bleeding lance and the Holy Grail, healing the blighted kingdom of the Fisher King. And after many years and many more adventures, when Parzival had grown into a wiser man, he did just as he had promised.

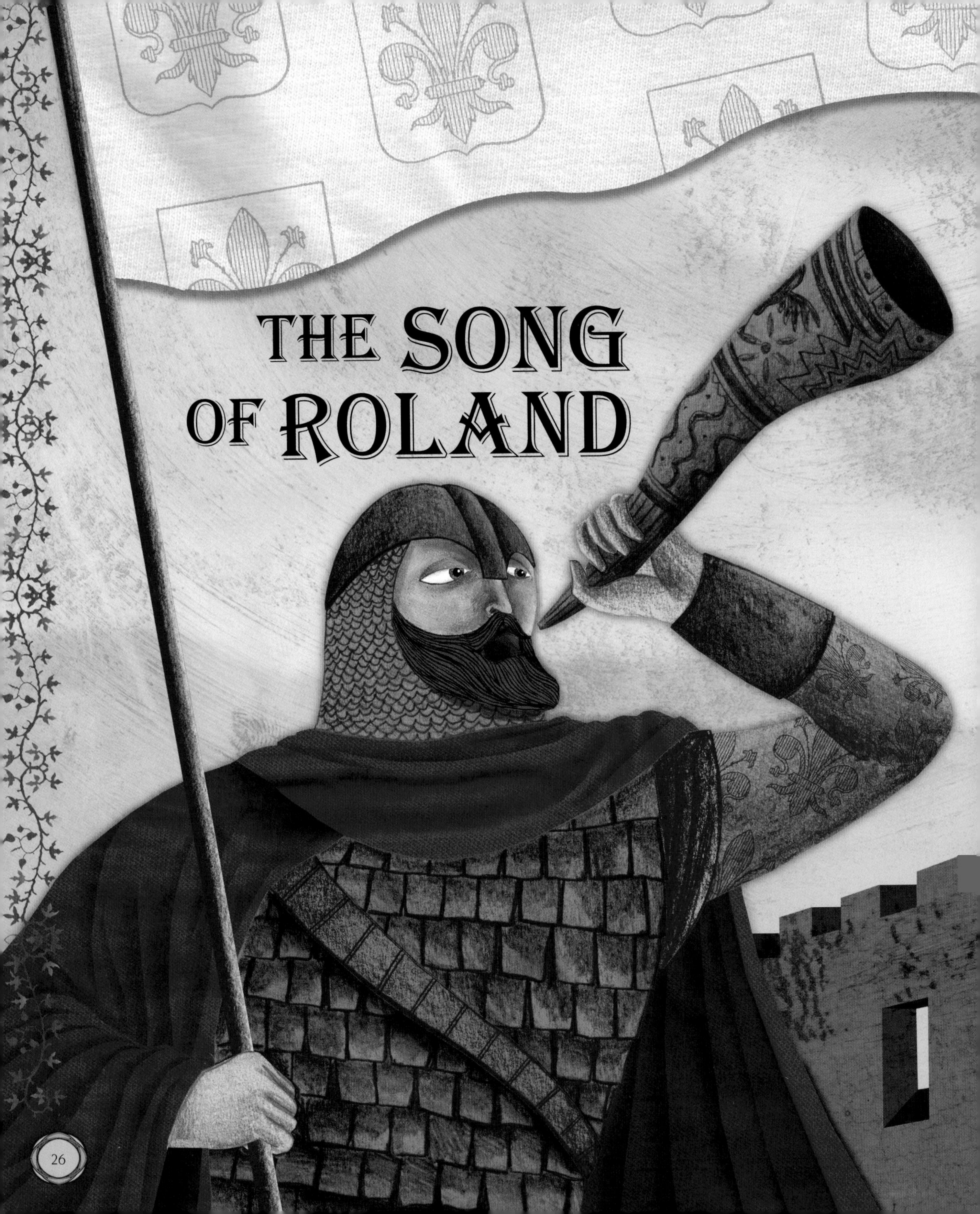

THE SONG OF ROLAND

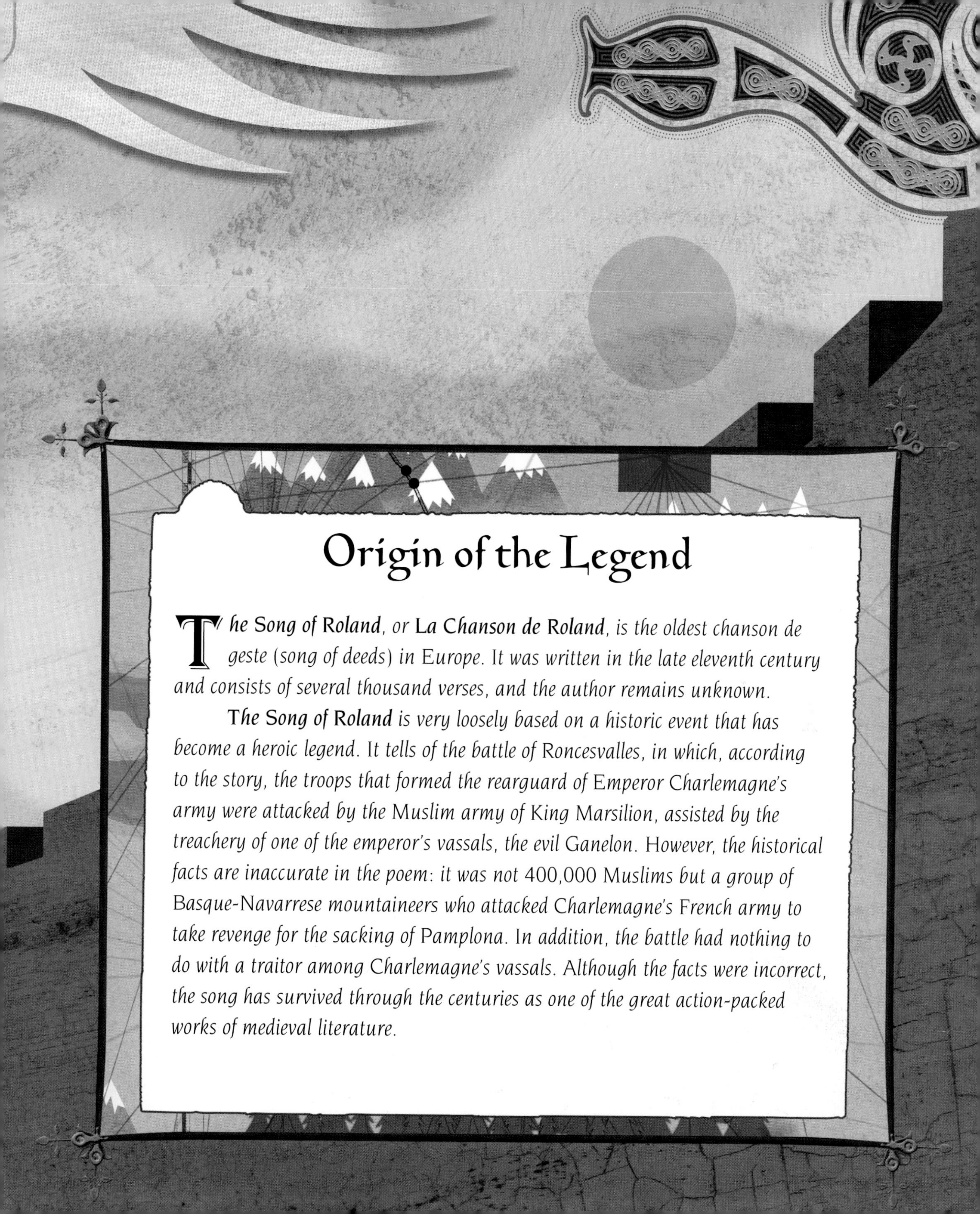

Origin of the Legend

The **Song of Roland**, *or* **La Chanson de Roland**, *is the oldest chanson de geste (song of deeds) in Europe. It was written in the late eleventh century and consists of several thousand verses, and the author remains unknown.*

The Song of Roland *is very loosely based on a historic event that has become a heroic legend. It tells of the battle of* Roncesvalles, *in which, according to the story, the troops that formed the rearguard of* Emperor Charlemagne's *army were attacked by the* Muslim *army of* King Marsilion, *assisted by the treachery of one of the emperor's vassals, the evil* Ganelon. *However, the historical facts are inaccurate in the poem: it was not* 400,000 Muslims *but a group of* Basque-Navarrese *mountaineers who attacked* Charlemagne's French *army to take revenge for the sacking of* Pamplona. *In addition, the battle had nothing to do with a traitor among* Charlemagne's *vassals. Although the facts were incorrect, the song has survived through the centuries as one of the great action-packed works of medieval literature.*

King Marsilion

Around the year 778, when the powerful Holy Roman Emperor Charlemagne had occupied Spain for seven years, there was only one place in the country left for him to conquer. This was the city of Saragossa, built up on a hill, and subject to King Marsilion.

One day Marsilion summoned his knights and spoke to them.

"Charlemagne has invaded this country and seeks our downfall. Give me counsel, wise men, since I know not what to do."

Blancandrín, one of the Moorish king's most cunning advisers, responded at once.

"Have no fear! Send Charlemagne a message of loyalty, together with all sorts of rich presents. Tell him that you have surrendered and that he can return in peace to France. Say that he may take with him some hostages from among your best men and that you yourself will go to France for the Feast of Saint Michael and will accept Charlemagne's Christian faith, giving up your own Muslim faith. Then when the date agreed upon arrives, you will not go. The emperor will kill the hostages in revenge for this ruse, but he will be too far away from Saragossa to make war on our people."

King Marsilion accepted this advice and sent ten men with olive branches, as signs of peace, to meet with Charlemagne.

The Emperor's Decision

When he received the messengers, Charlemagne felt hesitant; he was unsure he could trust King Marsilion. He called a council, bringing together his nobles and more than a thousand French knights.

Ganelon, an important knight who was also Charlemagne's brother-in-law, spoke up. "You would be guilty of the sin of pride if you did not accept the repentance of King Marsilion, who swears he will convert to the Christian faith."

"Ganelon's counsel is wise," said Naimon, one of the emperor's most faithful vassals. "King Marsilion has surrendered and it is logical that he asks your mercy. There is no reason to doubt him."

"Alas, my lord, if you trust Marsilion!" cried Roland, a beloved and brave knight who was Charlemagne's nephew and Ganelon's stepson. But when Charlemagne decided to trust King Marsilion, Roland was the first to offer to go to Saragossa with a message for Marsilion from the emperor.

"None of my twelve peers will go!" replied Charlemagne, remembering how Marsilion murdered a previous messenger. "Choose a baron of my dominions to do this."

"Send Ganelon," said Roland, who detested his stepfather.

Everyone supported the idea, and Ganelon burned with rage against Roland, since he feared King Marsilion and knew the mission was dangerous.

"If God permits me to come back, I will take my revenge," Ganelon threatened Roland before he left.

Ganelon's Treachery

Coming before King Marsilion, Ganelon gave him a false report of the emperor's message.

"If you accept the Christian faith, the king will give you half of Spain and give his nephew, Roland, the other half. If you do not accept this agreement you will be taken captive, you will be transported to Aachen, and there you will be tried and put to death."

Marsilion felt such anger on hearing this that he was on the point of killing Ganelon. But his wise councilor Blancandrín whispered to him that Ganelon might be willing to betray the emperor, so Marsilion made Ganelon a proposal.

"I will heap riches upon you for your entire life if you will tell me how I can defeat the great Charlemagne."

"The secret lies in defeating Roland, his friend Oliver, and the other twelve peers the king loves so much. And there only occurs to me one way to do this. When the king enters the narrow mountain paths of Cize, Roland and the other peers, and twenty thousand more Frenchmen, will remain in the rearguard. Send an army of a hundred thousand men and a hundred thousand after them. If you succeed in killing Roland, you will have taken away Charlemagne's right arm."

The deceitful Ganelon returned to his people and told them that Marsilion's repentance was sincere and that his whole army was fleeing. Charlemagne's army then set off for France, and Ganelon advised the king to put Roland in command of the rearguard.

Charlemagne did this, and when he caught sight of his own lands again, he wept in silence, because he had left behind his best men, among them Roland, the nephew he loved so much.

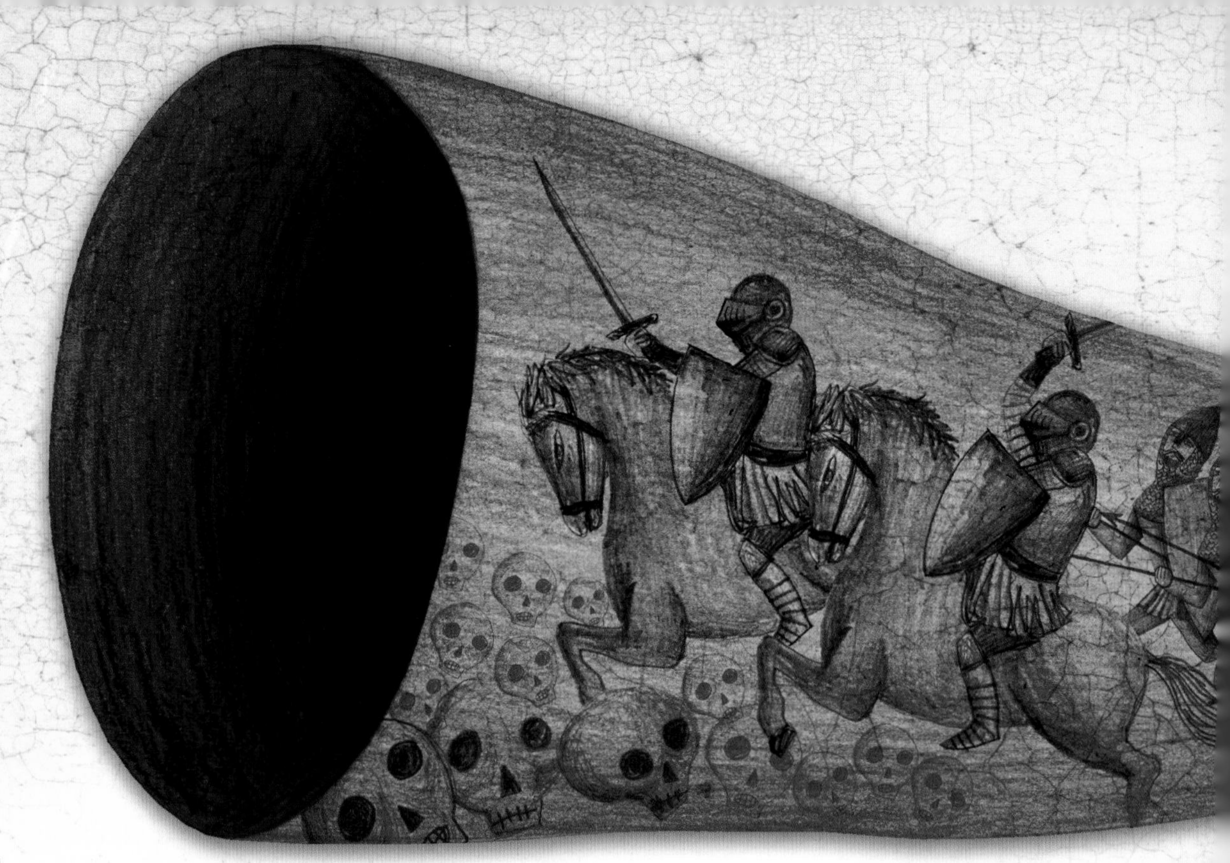

The Battle of Roncesvalles

Meanwhile, thousands of King Marsilion's men prepared to enter into battle to defend their land and their faith.

Charlemagne's rearguard suddenly heard the sound of a thousand trumpets. Oliver climbed a hill and from there observed an army of more than a hundred thousand men. Then he spoke to Roland.

"King Marsilion's army is uncountable and ours is very small. Roland, my friend, sound your horn. Charles will hear and return with the troops."

"By no means will I lose my renown in sweet France!"

"The troops of the Moors fill valleys, mountains, and plains. Blow your horn!"

"The enemy will not make me sound my horn!"

When the French saw the battle was near, their courage rose. They knew they would die, but before they did they would deal death to many in the opposing army.

The battle was great and terrible. The French fought valiantly, splitting the

shields of their enemies, shattering their helmets, and striking unerringly with swords and lances. "Montjoie!" the name of Charlemagne's sword, was their battle cry.

But the armies were terribly unequal in number and the twelve peers fell one by one, in spite of their courage.

When only seventy men were left among the French, Roland said, "I will sound my horn."

"If you had done so before we would have won the battle," his good friend Oliver replied, "but now it is too late."

Archbishop Turpin, also a man of great valor, spoke to the two of them.

"Blowing the horn will not save our lives, but it will bring the king back to avenge us. So do it."

Roland blew his horn so hard that his head ruptured and blood poured from his mouth.

When Charlemagne heard the sound of Roland's horn far in the distance, he froze. He knew that Roland and his best men were in danger. He also understood that Ganelon had betrayed them.

The Death of Roland

Bleeding, but still strong, the enraged Roland continued to fight even after the archbishop and Oliver were dead. He laid low twenty men, and four hundred joined to fight against him, shooting arrows at him with their bows, since none dared come close to him. He managed to slice off the right hand of King Marsilion.

Then the horns of the king of France were heard, and King Marsilion and his army fled.

But it was too late. Roland was fatally wounded from blowing his horn so powerfully. He gathered together as best he could the bodies of his best loved companions and began to weep. His sadness was so great that he could hardly stand. Then he sat down under a tree and died.

Vengeance

When the emperor reached Roncesvalles, he found not one of all those men he had loved so much alive. So great was his sorrow that for a few moments he thought he would go mad. But he managed to calm himself, since he knew that justice demanded that he take revenge.

A thousand knights were left to mourn the dead, while the rest left with him to pursue the army of the Moors. They caught up with them on the banks of the Ebro, and there, in a fierce battle, they defeated King Marsilion's army.

But vengeance did not end there, because Baligant, the Emir of Babylon, appeared with his army to fight against Charlemagne. And thus, in hand to hand combat, the king vanquished the emir.

But in spite of such a triumph, and Ganelon's eventual execution for his terrible betrayal, Charlemagne could not get over the pain he felt for the loss of his beloved valiant nephew Roland, and he wept for a great length of time into his white beard.

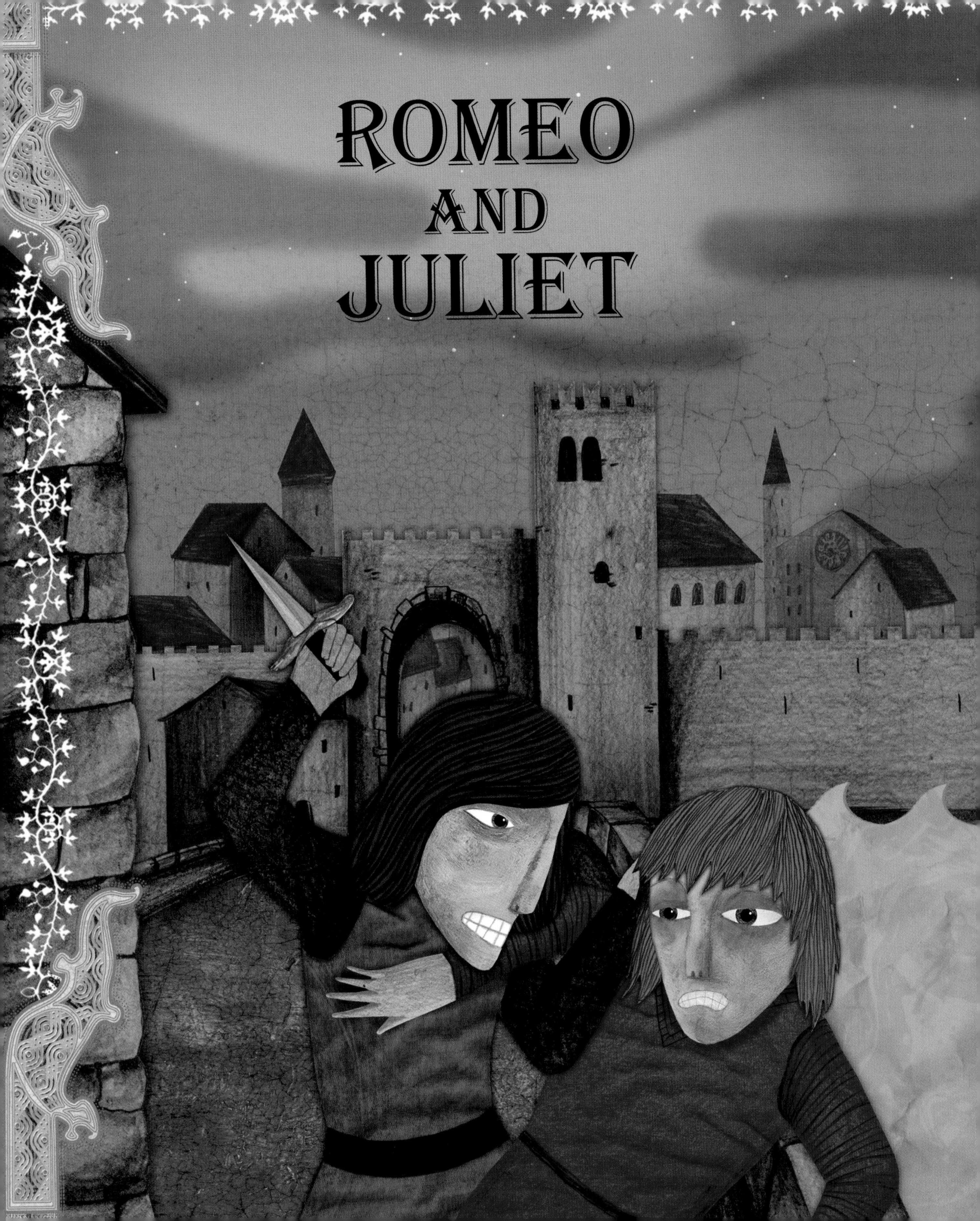
ROMEO
AND
JULIET

Origin of the Legend

Romeo and Juliet is perhaps the most famous love story of all time. The tragic tale about "star-crossed lovers" and their feuding families was written by the renowned English playwright William Shakespeare who was inspired by Arthur Brooke's 1562 poem, **The Tragical Historye of Romeus and Juliet** and William Painter's 1582 prose version, **Palace of Pleasure**. The story is based on a true story of two warring families that lived in Italy in the thirteenth century.

Shakespeare borrowed from Brooke and Painter, who themselves borrowed from the Italian poet Matteo Bandello's **Giuletta e Romeo**, but Shakespeare expanded the plot and made the characters more vivid. From its first performance in 1595, the play was a fabulous success because of the compelling tragic love story and Shakespeare's marvelous use of language.

In the Italian city of Verona today, you can visit a medieval tomb where it is said that the real Romeo and Juliet are buried.

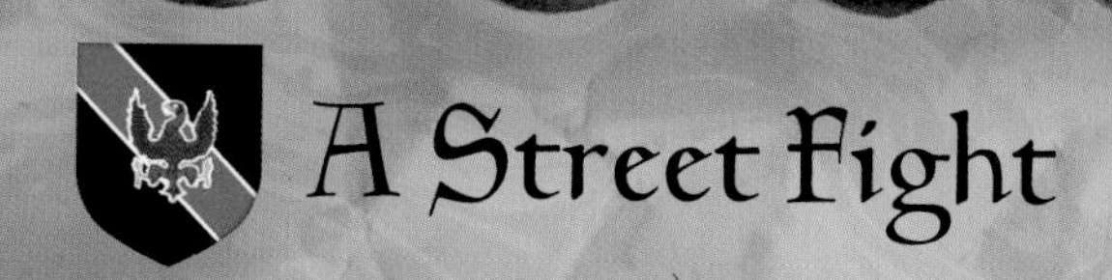

A Street Fight

In the Italian city of Verona, there were once two powerful families, the Montagues and the Capulets, who were archrivals. Every day members of each family fought each other in the streets.

One morning a young Montague named Benvolio, who was fed up with the constant feuding, saw two men sword-fighting. He stopped them and tried to make peace.

"Step back and put down your swords, fools!" he cried. "You know not what you do!"

Tybalt, of the Capulet family, challenged him, sneering, "Come here Benvolio, and look upon your death!"

The street was soon filled with insults, threats, and the swords of supporters of the Montagues and the Capulets, until a group of citizens and officers separated the warring families.

A Young Man in Love

When tempers had cooled off, Benvolio's cousin appeared, a handsome young man named Romeo, who looked very melancholy.

"What's the matter, Romeo?" Benvolio asked. "Are you perhaps in love?"

Romeo was indeed in love with a girl named Rosaline, but she had just rejected him, telling him she did not want the love of any man.

Benvolio tried to cheer him up. "Be ruled by me, forget to think of her," he said.

"O teach me how I should forget to think," Romeo replied, skeptically.

"By giving liberty unto your eyes to examine other beauties."

But Romeo could imagine no woman lovelier than Rosaline. Benvolio remembered that Lord Capulet was hosting a great ball that evening. He and Romeo, being Montagues, were forbidden to attend any party of the Capulets. But this was a special party: a masked ball. In disguise, Benvolio realized, they would be able to sneak in and Romeo could then observe the beauty of the other women of Verona. Romeo only agreed to go so that he could see his beloved Rosaline.

At the Party

Romeo, Benvolio, and another friend, the witty Mercutio, put on masks and went to the Capulet's party.

Very soon, Romeo saw a lady so beautiful he completely forgot about Rosaline. He approached her and quickly won her heart, though they spoke for only a few minutes. Then he learned, much to his dismay, that she was none other than Juliet, the daughter of Lord Capulet himself.

Juliet was also surprised to learn the identity of the handsome young man she had just met. Her beloved Nurse, the servant who had cared for her all her life, cautioned her, “His name is Romeo, and a Montague, the only son of your great enemy.”

Juliet gasped. “My only love sprung from my only hate!”

Juliet's Balcony

On his way home that night, Romeo climbed over the Capulets' wall.

He found Juliet leaning on her balcony, weeping. "O Romeo, Romeo!" she cried. "'Tis but your name that is my enemy. What's Montague? O, be some other name! What's in a name? That which we call a rose by any other name would smell as sweet."

Romeo called up to Juliet from the darkness below, "I'll be new baptized! Henceforth I never will be Romeo!"

Juliet was startled and worried to see him there. But at the same time his declaration of love filled her with joy.

She made a pact with Romeo: "If your love be honorable and your purpose marriage, send me word tomorrow where and what time thou wilt perform the rite."

The Secret Wedding

At dawn, Romeo went to the church of Friar Lawrence, told the kind priest all about Juliet, and asked if he would allow them to marry in secret. The friar hoped their love might end their families' bitter feud, and so he agreed to hold a private ceremony.

Romeo gave a message to Juliet's Nurse, who was the only other person who knew of their secret. "Go to Friar Lawrence's cell," the Nurse told Juliet. "There stays a husband to make you a wife!"

A Sad Goodbye

That day Romeo and Juliet were secretly married, and they each had to go their separate ways. Soon after, Romeo saw Tybalt, Juliet's cousin, kill his friend Mercutio in a street fight. He was so enraged by the murder of his friend that he took revenge on Tybalt, stabbing him in a deadly duel.

Romeo escaped the police and hid in the friar's church. The Nurse helped him sneak into Juliet's room so they could see each other one more time before Romeo had to leave Verona for good. When dawn came, the young husband and wife had to say goodbye.

"Oh my love, will you be going now? It is not yet near day," pleaded Juliet.

"I must be gone and live, or stay and die."

"Oh, shall we ever meet again?" Juliet asked.

"I doubt it not," Romeo reassured her. And so he left for the town of Mantua, where he hoped Juliet would one day join him.

Juliet's mother then came in with terrible news for her daughter. The Capulets had decided to marry her off to a nobleman, Count Paris, in just two days. Juliet—who, of course, could not tell her mother she was already married to Romeo—refused, but her father insisted. He was so determined to marry her to Paris that he threatened to disown her if she did not obey.

"If you will not wed," Lord Capulet thundered, "hang, beg, starve, die in the streets, for I'll never acknowledge you again."

The Friar's Plan

Juliet played along, but ran to the friar for advice on how to stop the unwanted wedding, which would take her away from Romeo forever. "O bid me leap from any tower," she pleaded, "rather than marry Paris."

Friar Lawrence proposed a cunning plan. He gave Juliet a potion to take that night that would put her to sleep for two days—a sleep so deep she would appear dead. Then, the next morning, her family would bury her in the family tomb. The friar would later bring Romeo back from Mantua in time for Juliet to wake up. The two lovers could then escape and live in secret together.

Juliet agreed to carry out this dangerous plan. The next morning, the Capulets wept to find their daughter dead—or so they thought—and her wedding was replaced with a funeral.

A Lost Letter

Meanwhile, Friar Lawrence sent a messenger to Mantua with a letter for Romeo that explained the plan. But the messenger was not allowed to pass the city gates out of fear of a contagious plague. So Romeo never got the letter.

Unfortunately, another friend of Romeo's, hearing the Capulets' news, told him Juliet was dead. Since Romeo did not know the truth, he was so devastated that he no longer wanted to live. He obtained a poison and returned to Verona, seeking out the Capulets' tomb. There he would drink the poison and die by Juliet's side, to be with her forever. "Juliet, I will lie with you tonight!" he vowed.

A Tragic End

When Friar Lawrence heard that Romeo never got his message, he rushed to the tomb to get Juliet out. But when he arrived, he saw that he had come too late. Romeo had already broken into the tomb, and seeing Juliet's apparently lifeless body, he had drunk the deadly poison and died in her arms. Sadly, Juliet's potion wore off only moments later. When she woke up and found the corpse of her beloved beside her, she did not want to live without him. She took Romeo's dagger from his belt and stabbed herself.

The Capulets and Montagues were horrified to find their children lying dead together in the tomb. When Friar Lawrence explained to them the whole story, they were ashamed for the tragedy their feuding had brought upon themselves. The two families and the whole city mourned the lovers and pledged to live in peace.

"For never was a story of more woe," they said, "than this of Juliet and her Romeo."

YVAIN,
THE KNIGHT
OF THE LION

Origin of the Legend

Yvain, the **Knight** *of the* **Lion***, was written by the French court poet Chrétien de Troyes in the late twelfth century, around the same time he wrote* **Lancelot, the Knight of the Cart***. The story has many supernatural elements in it, including an enchanted storm-creating fountain, a magic ring, a fire-breathing serpent, and a loyal lion.*

Yvain, the Knight of the Lion *is a tale of chivalry about one of the knights of King Arthur's Round Table. In this Arthurian romance, Yvain's courageous exploits are detailed, as well as his successful attempt to win back the love of the wife he left behind for a life of adventure. Yvain was one of the earliest characters associated with King Arthur, as well as one of the most popular. In Welsh mythology he is known as Owain or Owein, and the Welsh legend,* **Owain***, or* **The Lady of the Fountain***, is very similar to Chrétien's tale.*

Calogrenant's Adventure

One day at Camelot, when King Arthur had brought together his knights for a good meal, a courteous knight named Calogrenant told an unsettling and wondrous tale.

Having gone out in search of adventure in the forest of Brocéliande, Calogrenant came upon a man who told him how he could put his bravery to the test. Nearby was a fountain underneath a beautiful tree from which a pitcher hung. On one side of the fountain was a hermitage and on the other a great stone.

"If you take water from the fountain," the man said, "and pour it on the stone, you will see the most terrible storm you could ever imagine."

Calogrenant hurried off to find the enchanted fountain and pour water on the great stone. But he soon had reason to regret what he had done, because he thought he would not survive the savage storm.

When the storm was over and he found, to his surprise,that he was still alive, a fierce knight appeared to challenge him. As the strange knight was much stronger than Calogrenant, he knocked him to the ground and took Calogrenant's horse, leaving him humiliated.

On hearing this tale, Yvain, Calogrenant's fearless cousin, was enraged. "I will avenge this insult, Calogrenant."

However, King Arthur decided that some days later he himself, along with those who might wish to accompany him, would go to see the fountain and its marvelous powers.

Yvain and the Knight of the Fountain

Yvain, who preferred to fight alone, decided to leave first without telling anyone. He rode until he came to the fountain and the tree. He poured the water from the pitcher over the great stone and in an instant he was witness to the brutal storm.

When the knight arrived to challenge him, both fought fiercely. Finally, Yvain struck a fatal blow, and his opponent, bleeding badly, fled to his castle. Yvain followed him as fast as he could, since he wished to take some proof of his victory. The knight went through the castle gate, but when Yvain was passing through it his horse stepped on a beam that sprung a trap, and an iron door fell, cutting the animal in half.

Beyond that door was another iron door that also came down, leaving Yvain caught in a mysterious room.

The Maiden and the Ring

Then there came a maiden who recognized Yvain immediately, since he had once come to her aid.

"My lord is dead, and everyone in the palace wants to kill you for that. But I am Lunete, whom you once helped, and I will not let anything bad happen to you. Put on this magic ring. When you wear it you will become invisible."

Yvain did this, and when several knights and the widow entered the room to take their revenge they could find no one.

When Yvain caught sight of the dead knight's widow, Laudine, he thought her the most beautiful woman in the world, and immediately fell in love with her.

Lunete, seeing Yvain so enamored, proposed to intervene with the lady in his favor. In a few days she had convinced the lady that the fountain could not be left unprotected and that the man who had killed her lord must necessarily be a nobler knight than her lord.

Laudine realized that Yvain had done no more than defend himself. She pardoned him and they soon married happily.

The Love Pact

When King Arthur and his knights reached the fountain they discovered that Yvain had become the lord of the palace nearby. He welcomed them and together they spent many contented days.

But when the time came for them to leave, Sir Gawain, a cousin and dear friend of Yvain's, convinced him to go with them, since a knight should never give up seeking adventure.

Yvain asked his lady's permission to go, and with great sorrow Laudine gave it to him, but she warned him that if he were not back within a year she would never forgive him and he would lose her love forever.

He swore to return before the year was up and rode off, suffering for leaving his beloved.

Yvain's Madness

Yvain and Gawain had many adventures and lost track of time. One day at King Arthur's court a maiden spoke to Yvain: "You have betrayed my lady and now she no longer loves you. She orders you never to dare try to return to her side."

Yvain realized that he had failed in his promise and felt a pain so intense he left the palace and fled to the forest. There he spent weeks living like a lunatic and getting weaker and weaker, until some maidens found him, naked and out of his mind, and took him to the castle where they lived. Once there they gave him every care, and he soon recovered his strength and his senses.

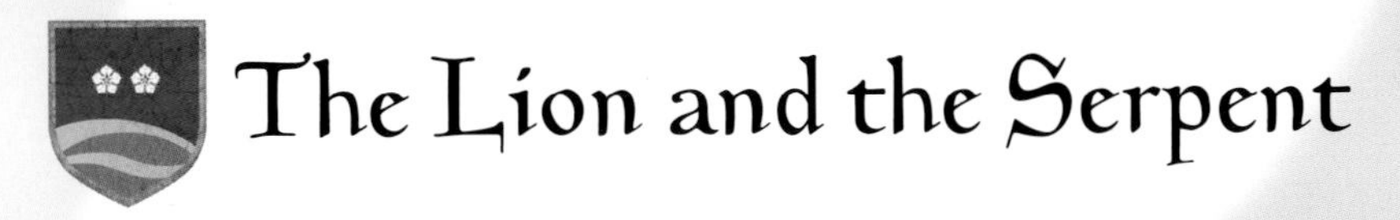

The Lion and the Serpent

After paying his debt to the lady of the castle by vanquishing a count who had been terrorizing her, Yvain took his leave.

Once back in the forest he came upon a serpent that had seized a lion in its coils and was burning its back with the flames that shot out of its mouth.

Yvain decided to help the lion. He slashed the serpent in two with one stroke of his sword, freeing the wild beast. Then the lion bowed his head and knelt before him with all the humility and gratitude of a noble knight.

Yvain set out on his way again, followed by the lion, which from that time on never left his side. The lion became Yvain's loyal protector.

Prisoner in the Hermitage

One day Yvain and his lion reached the magic fountain, and there they heard the sorrowful weeping of a captive shut up in the hermitage. It was Lunete.

"Three knights have accused me of treason for having aided my lord Yvain, and tomorrow I am to burn at the stake!" she cried.

"My dear Lunete," he replied, "I swear that tomorrow I will save you from the stake. But if anyone asks, tell them I am the Knight of the Lion."

The following day, after defeating a terrible giant, Yvain quickly vanquished the three knights who had accused Lunete. Lunete did not reveal Yvain's identity and no one recognized him, but were left quite amazed by his enormous skill and valor.

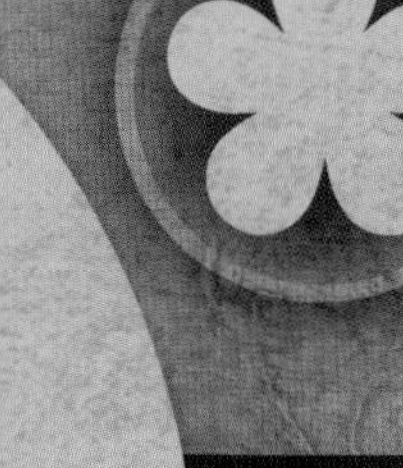

The Two Sisters and their Lawsuit

While the fame of the Knight of the Lion kept growing, two sisters began a lawsuit. The older sister wished to deny the younger sister her part of their inheritance. First the older woman came to King Arthur's court and asked Gawain to defend her cause. When the younger one came as well, the king set a date by which she was to find someone to defend her, and the younger sister set off in search of the Knight of the Lion.

In this way, destiny so designed that Gawain and Yvain, not recognizing one another in their helmets and armor, would meet in combat. Both fought with such skill that after hours of battle Yvain declared, "Never have I known a knight of such extraordinary valor, and for that reason I consider myself vanquished."

"Vanquished am I, noble sir, since I can scarcely stand. You have in me, Gawain, an admirer."

"If I had recognized you I would never have entered into this combat, since I am Yvain, who loves you more than any other knight in the entire world!"

The two friends embraced, deeply moved, and left the decision as to the lawsuit of the two sisters in the hands of the king.

The king wished to do justice and decided in favor of the younger daughter. Afterward the whole court celebrated Yvain's return.

His Lady's Pardon

Some days later, Yvain again departed, determined to obtain his lady's forgiveness.

Meanwhile, Lunete convinced Laudine that she needed a knight to defend the fountain and that the best knight for the task was the Knight of the Lion. When the knight had saved Lunete from being burned at the stake, the lady had asked him to stay in her castle. But Yvain had answered that he would not do so until he obtained the pardon of his beloved.

Lunete had cleverly persuaded her lady to swear that if she brought the Knight of the Lion to her, she would do all she could to make his lady pardon him.

Laudine vowed to do so and when Yvain knelt before her and confessed who he was, she had no choice but to pardon him. Having passed all the tests, Yvain succeeded in regaining the love of his lady and they lived together happily.

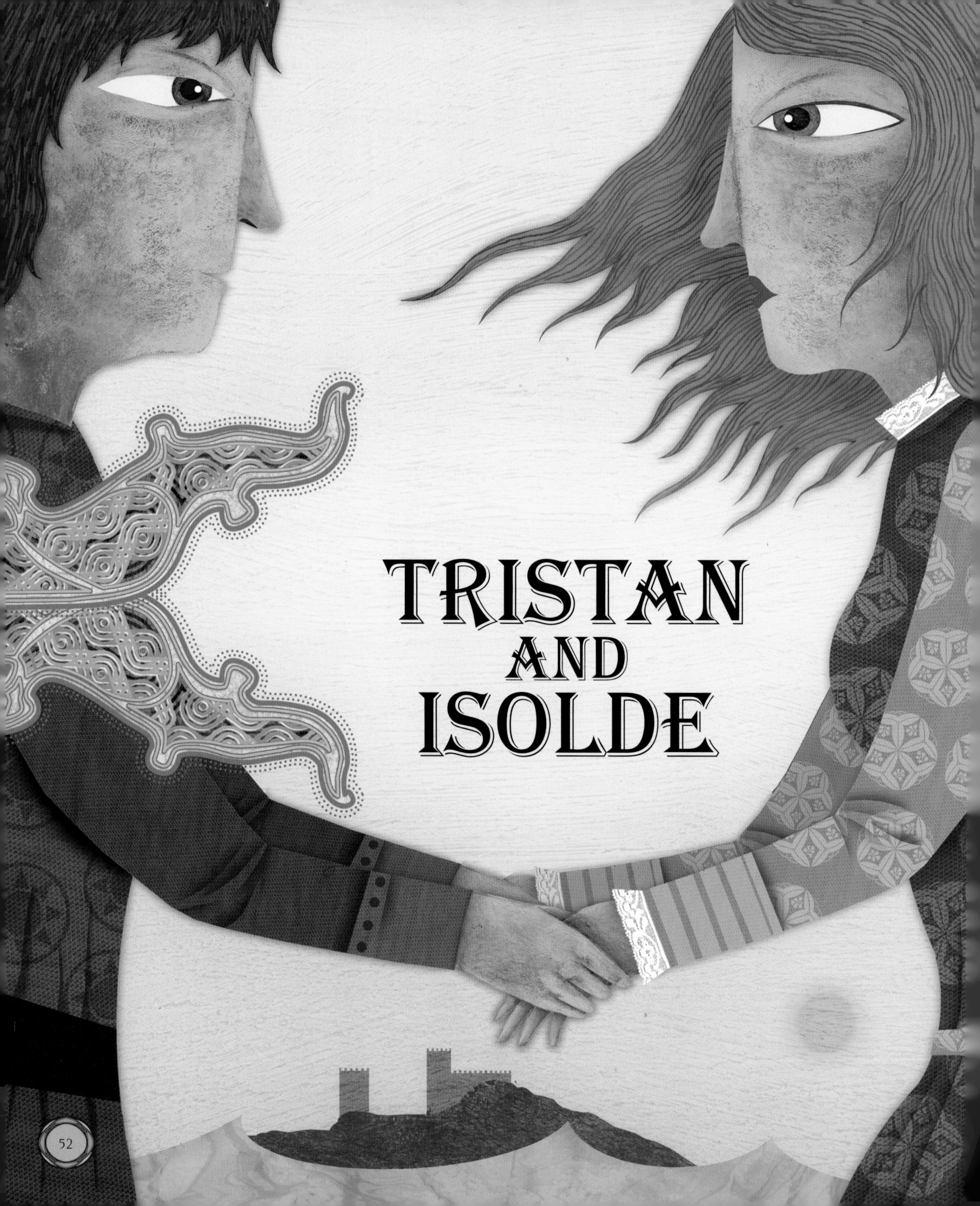

TRISTAN AND ISOLDE

Origin of the Legend

Tristan and Isolde, *like* Romeo and Juliet, *is one of the greatest romantic tragedies ever written. This medieval legend tells the tragic love story of Tristan, a heroic warrior; Isolde, a healer; and King Mark of Cornwall, Tristan's uncle. Not only is it a tale of romance, but also one of loyalty, jealousy, and the forces of fate.*

Many authors wrote versions of the tale, which combines Celtic, Irish, Welsh, and Breton sources. The most famous authors include the French poets Béroul and Thomas of Briton, and later on, Eilhart von Oberg and Gottfried van Strassburg. **Tristan and Isolde** *was one of the most influential romances of the Middle Ages, inspiring the later Arthurian romance of Lancelot and Guinevere. Originally, the legend had nothing to do with King Arthur, but by the thirteenth century, written works held that Tristan was one of the knights of the Round Table, linking the legends together forevermore.*

Tristan's Victory Over Morholt

When the noble Blancheflor, sister of Mark, King of Cornwall, gave birth to her son, she was very sad, because her husband had just been killed in battle. Therefore she decided to name her child Tristan, which means "sadness."

Every five years, Cornwall was forced by Ireland to hand over a tribute of three hundred young men and women as slaves. This was the demand of the Irish king, enforced by the evil Morholt, a fierce warrior who was more like a giant than a man.

No knight had ever dared to meet him in battle, until Tristan came to his uncle's aid and challenged Morholt to single combat. After a long, arduous battle, Tristan defeated him.

Tristan returned to Cornwall, but unfortunately, he sustained terrible wounds from Morholt's poisoned sword. Near death, Tristan sailed to distant lands in search of a remedy, since no one in his own country could cure him. As fate would have it, he landed again on the coast of Ireland, where some fishermen found him. They took Tristan to the Irish queen and her lovely daughter, Isolde, for they were experts in the art of healing.

When his wound was healed Tristan returned to Cornwall.

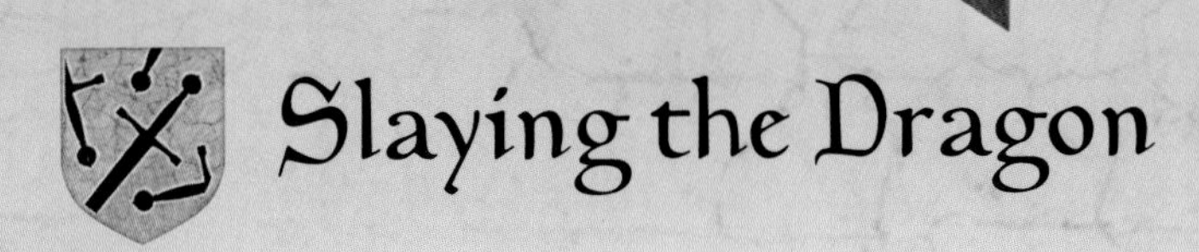

Slaying the Dragon

Everyone was happy about Tristan's return to Cornwall, except some knights who envied Tristan because he enjoyed King Mark's favor.

Since the king had no children, he considered Tristan to be the heir to the throne. The knights urged the king to marry, so there would be other princes and princesses to inherit the kingdom. One day when the king was alone in his chamber, two swallows flew in through the window and placed a strand of hair—radiant as a ray of sunlight—in his hands.

King Mark then summoned his court. "Only the princess whose hair this is shall be my wife," he declared.

Tristan recognized the hair. It was Isolde's, the princess of Ireland. He swore to the king that he would find her. But when he arrived in Ireland, he learned that a dragon was terrorizing the people. The Irish king offered the hand of Isolde in marriage to whoever could destroy the dragon.

Tristan, in disguise, hunted the dragon and slew it. Isolde once again cured his wounds. When the king offered to give her to him as his wife, Tristan revealed his true identity and convinced him that the girl should marry his uncle so that Ireland and Cornwall might end their conflicts.

Isolde was devastated to be leaving her people for a foreign land and a husband-to-be whom she did not know.

Love Potion

Before the journey, the Irish queen wanted to make sure Isolde's marriage would be happy so she gave a powerful love potion to her daughter's maid, Bragnae, and told her to drop it into the drinks of Isolde and the King of Cornwall on their wedding night, to make sure they would love each other.

But during the voyage to Cornwall, when the weather was hot, and Tristan was trying to console the homesick Isolde, he asked Bragnae to bring him and Isolde something to drink. By mistake, she gave them the magical love potion.

Immediately upon drinking it, Tristan and Isolde fell deeply in love, despite the fact that Isolde was destined to marry Tristan's uncle.

Forbidden Love

The King of Cornwall's wedding with Isolde went ahead as planned. But Tristan and Isolde continued to see each other secretly.

One of the knights who envied Tristan saw the two lovers together one night. He rushed to tell the others what he had seen and together they went to report this treachery to the king.

The king agreed to set a trap for his nephew. He told Tristan he had to travel to England the next day to deliver a letter to King Arthur's court, knowing that if he really were in love with Isolde he would want to say goodbye to her before his journey. Sure enough, that night the king discovered his wife and his nephew together.

Enraged, the king arrested Tristan and Isolde for their betrayal and sentenced them to be burned at the stake.

Flight to the Forest

When guards were taking Tristan to the stake he used a trick to escape. He begged them to allow him to enter a chapel to pray. The guards let him, since the chapel had only one door and a window that overlooked a cliff. No one would have dared to jump out of it—no one but Tristan.

Isolde had been given a harsher punishment than burning: she was thrown into a pit of diseased lepers whose infection would cause a painfully slow death. But once Tristan survived his leap over the cliff, he came back to rescue her. He fought off the lepers and fled with Isolde into the forest.

The Pardon

The two lovers lived for several years in the forest, enduring all sorts of hardships. Sometimes they took refuge in caves, but most of the time they just wandered, foraging for mushrooms and berries.

After a while, Tristan could no longer bear seeing Isolde suffer. So he disguised himself and returned to his uncle's castle to swear to Isolde's innocence. He asked that Isolde be pardoned of all crimes and said that he would defend her honor—in a duel—against anyone in the court who still accused her.

None of the king's knights dared fight this mysterious stranger. Impressed, the king agreed to take Isolde back, since he still loved her very much. But he declared that Tristan would still not be welcome in the castle.

With great sorrow Tristan took leave of his beloved. She gave him a ring and pledged a solemn oath to him: "Take this ring. If you ever send a messenger to bring it to me, I will come to your side."

Isolde of the White Hands

A heartbroken Tristan crossed the English Channel and arrived in the lands of Brittany of northern France. After defeating a powerful count who was laying siege to the city, he won the favor of the local king, who offered him the hand of his daughter in marriage. Tristan's heart was still with Isolde, but because he was convinced that his beloved no longer remembered him, he agreed to marry again. By coincidence, his new bride was also named Isolde—Isolde of the White Hands.

But his continuing love for the first Isolde made it impossible for Tristan to love his new wife.

After another battle where he was wounded with a poisoned sword, he knew that only the first Isolde could save him from death. So he told the King of Brittany his whole tragic story and begged him to go to Cornwall in search of her, taking the ring she had given him.

"Take my ship and two sails," he told the king. "If Isolde is with you when you return, raise the white one. If she is not with you, raise the black."

Alas, Isolde of the White Hands had been listening at the door and overheard their conversation with great jealousy.

Tristan's Final Hour

Upon hearing of Tristan's fatal wounds, Queen Isolde set sail that same night. The white sail was hoisted, as Tristan had instructed.

Tristan's wife came to tell him that the ship was approaching.

"What color is the sail they've raised?" Tristan asked.

"The sail," she lied, "is black."

"I die for you, my beloved Isolde!" Tristan cried. "You did not take pity on my wounds. At least you will weep for my death."

When Queen Isolde arrived she found all the people of Brittany mourning for Tristan's death. She felt such sorrow that she lay down beside his body, embraced him once more, and died for love of him.

When King Mark learned what had happened, he forgave Tristan and had the two tragic lovers buried together. It is said that from Tristan's grave a vine grew, while from Isolde's grew a rose, and the two plants intertwined, symbolizing their eternal love.

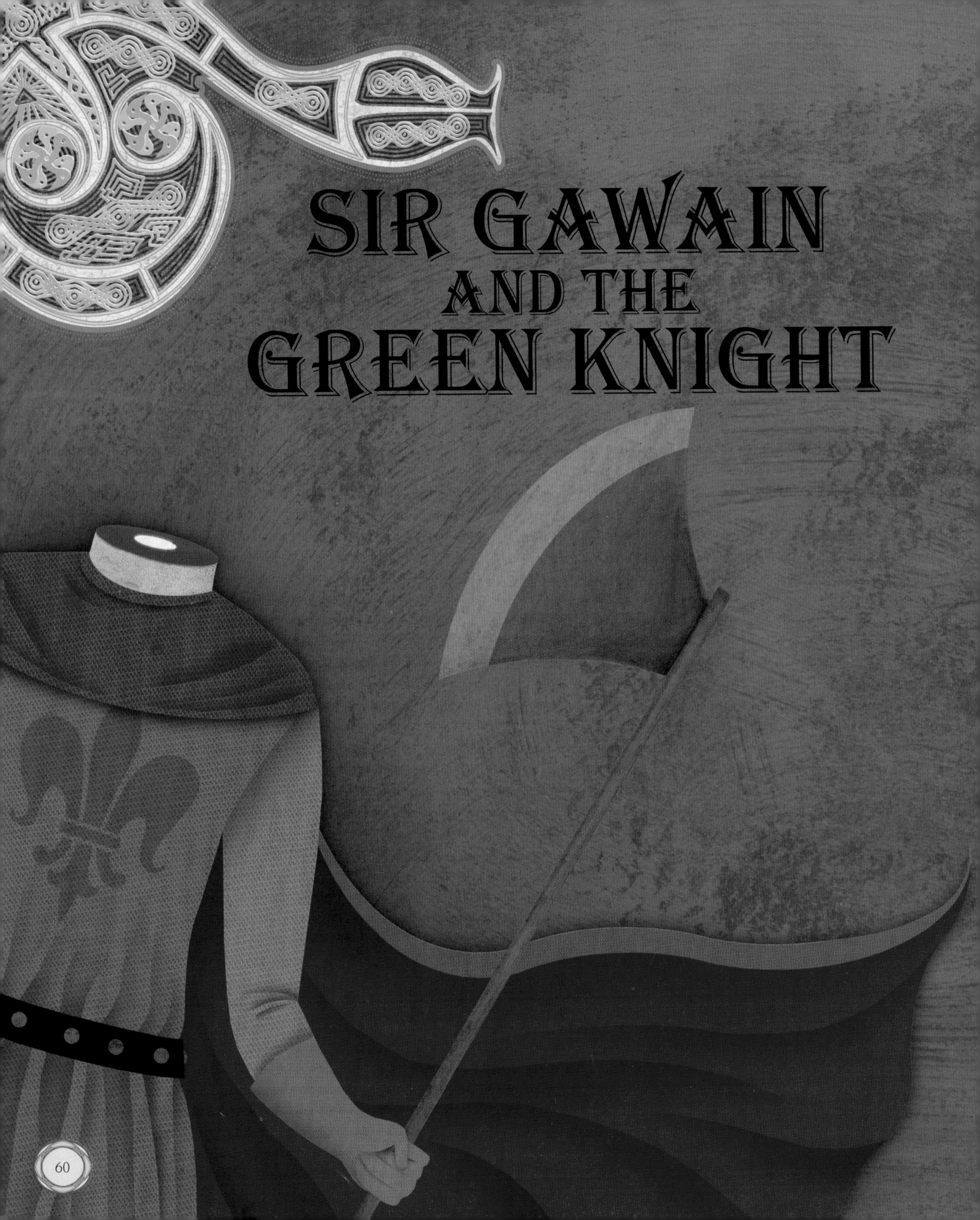

SIR GAWAIN AND THE GREEN KNIGHT

Origin of the Legend

Sir ***Gawain and the Green Knight****, a romance of the late fourteenth century, is one of the best known and most frequently read medieval tales of England. The poem survives within a single manuscript, along with three other religious texts called* ***Pearl, Patience****, and* ***Purity****. These four narrative poems are all written in Middle English. The author remains unknown and is sometimes called the "Pearl poet."*

The legend tells the adventures of Sir Gawain, one of the knights of King Arthur's Round Table, who accepts a strange challenge from an unknown warrior dressed all in green.

One of the themes in the story is that of beheading, a subject that is recurrent in Celtic mythology, which probably served as the original inspiration for this unusual legend.

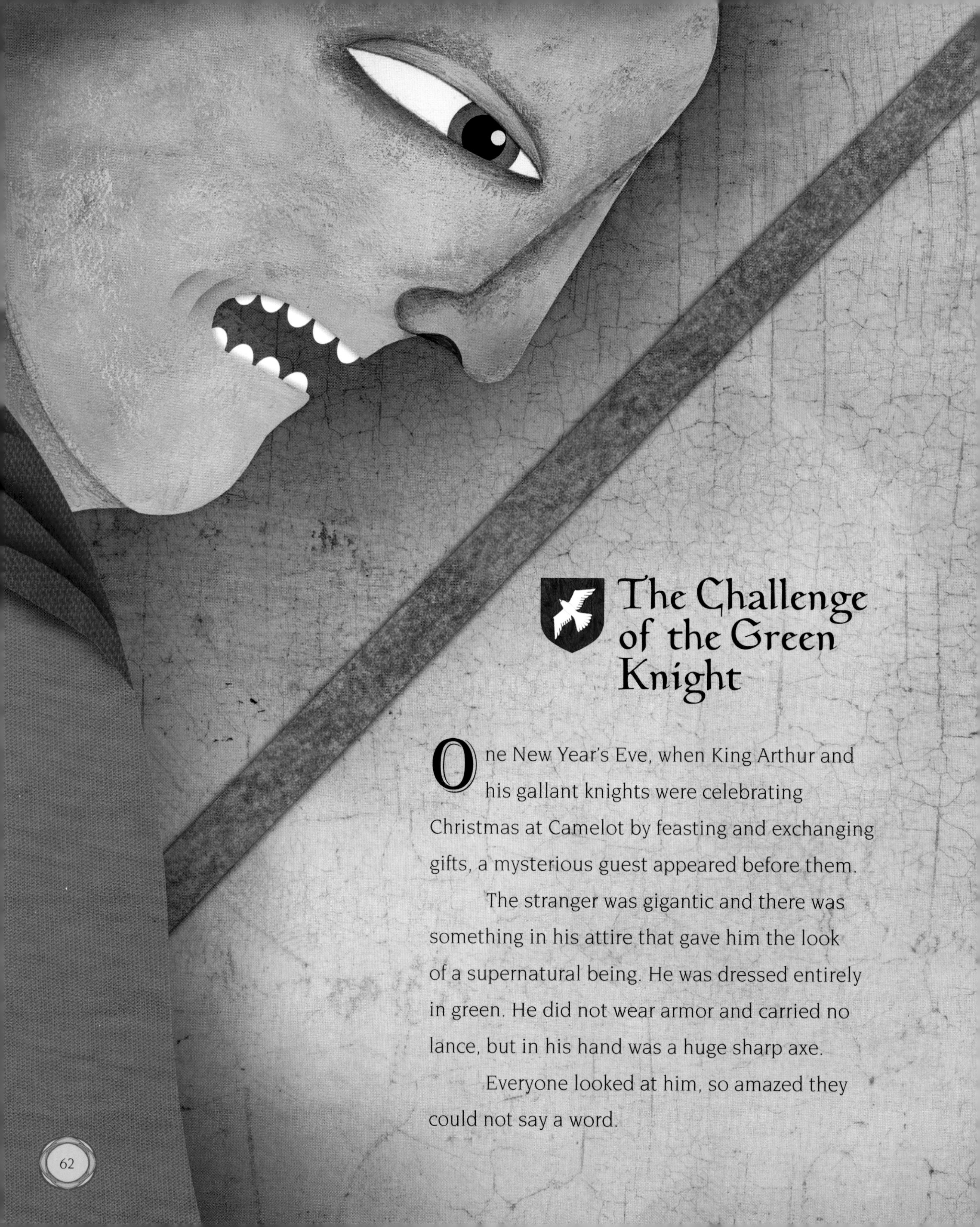

The Challenge of the Green Knight

One New Year's Eve, when King Arthur and his gallant knights were celebrating Christmas at Camelot by feasting and exchanging gifts, a mysterious guest appeared before them.

The stranger was gigantic and there was something in his attire that gave him the look of a supernatural being. He was dressed entirely in green. He did not wear armor and carried no lance, but in his hand was a huge sharp axe.

Everyone looked at him, so amazed they could not say a word.

"I know that this is the court of King Arthur," he announced, "and they say that here the bravest and most noble knights are to be found. I want one of them to accept my challenge. I dare any one of those present to take my axe and strike me with all their strength. I will receive the blow without moving and then I will go. I will give that knight exactly one year and a day to come and find me, wherever I might be, and let me give him back the blow, since that is just."

King Arthur finally spoke. "Sir, what you ask is madness, but since you so obstinately seek it, you deserve to find it. Give me the axe."

Gawain's Blow

But at that moment, Sir Gawain, Arthur's nephew, stepped in.

"I cannot permit you to accept this challenge. I beg you to leave it to me, since if I lose, my life will not be mourned like yours would be. Let the knights of the court decide."

The rest of the knights considered the virtuous Gawain's request a sensible one, so he took the axe and raised the weapon, preparing to let it fall. The Green Knight bowed his head, showing his bare neck. Gawain hit him with the sharp blade and the axe sunk into the Green Knight's flesh and cut off his head in one blow.

Everyone gasped, speechless with terror, as the Green Knight stood up and picked his great head up off the ground. Then he held the head up high and it spoke to Gawain.

"If you dare keep your promise and do not wish to be known as a coward, in a year and a day seek out the Green Chapel. There you will find me and receive a blow like the one you gave to me."

The strange Green Knight then rode swiftly out of the castle, with his enormous head still in his hands.

Gawain and the Lord of the Castle

The year passed swiftly and soon it was time for Gawain to go in search of the terrible knight. He rode through forests and across mountains with no other company than his horse. Everywhere he went he asked about the Green Knight, but no one knew anything about him.

One cold day he found himself deep in a forest, wishing he could find shelter. Suddenly he saw a castle of great beauty and approached it.

Gawain was given a splendid welcome by the lord of the castle, Bertilak de Hautdesert, who insisted that he put off his departure. When Gawain told Bertilak he had to reach the Green Chapel before New Year's Day, the lord laughed, replying that the chapel was nearby and that on the appointed day he would show Gawain the way there. And then the lord made a proposal.

"While you are here you will spend the day at home, resting. I, on the other hand, will go out hunting, and at the end of the day we will exchange what we have found."

That agreement seemed quite extraordinary to Gawain, but since he wished to show his appreciation to the lord of the castle, he gratefully accepted Lord Bertilak's bargain.

Temptation

The following day Bertilak and a group of his men went out hunting. Meanwhile, Gawain was sleeping in his chamber when suddenly he heard the door open. The lord's wife, Lady Bertilak, who was the most beautiful lady that he had ever seen, more beautiful even than Queen Guinevere, walked in and sat down on the edge of his bed.

Gawain acted as if he were still asleep, then pretended to wake up, very surprised. The lady began to flirt with him, while the knight was evasive, though without at any moment failing to be polite.

When about to say goodbye the lady told him that a courteous knight could not be with a lady so long without asking her for a kiss. So Gawain asked her for a kiss and the lady delicately leaned forward and gave him one.

That night the lord of the castle kept his part of the bargain, giving Gawain the deer he had taken in the hunt. Gawain, for his part, put his arms around the lord's neck and gave him a kiss, since that was what he had obtained that day. They agreed that the following day, no matter what happened, they would again exchange their trophies.

The Magic Sash

What happened the next day was not very different. The lord of the castle, after a hard day's hunting, brought Gawain a magnificent wild boar. Gawain, in turn, firmly but chivalrously resisted the wiles of his host's wife and at the end of the day gave him the two kisses that the lady had given him. The knight insisted they repeat the game once again.

The following morning the lady went further than ever in her attempts at seduction, begging Gawain to accept a token of her love. She took off the girdle, or sash, she was wearing around her waist and gave it to him.

"There is no man under the sun that can do any harm to the knight who wears this green sash, since it is magic and whoever wears it cannot die in any earthly way."

It occurred to Gawain that the sash could save his life when he found himself before the Knight of the Green Chapel. He accepted it, along with the three kisses the lady gave him.

That evening when they made their exchange, Lord Bertilak gave Gawain a fox he had hunted and Gawain gave Lord Bertilak three kisses. Gawain said nothing, however, about the magic sash, keeping it for himself.

Gawain at the Green Chapel

The next day Gawain set out for the Green Chapel. When he arrived he found the terrible Green Knight sharpening an axe that appeared even more fearsome than the one Gawain had used to cut off his head with one blow.

As had been arranged, Gawain took off his helmet and bowed his head to receive the blow of the axe.

When the axe was about to hit his neck, he trembled and the Green Knight pulled up the weapon, accusing him of cowardice. Gawain swore that he would not flinch again.

The knight raised the axe once more and, wild with fury, struck his blow, but he did not even manage to graze him.

Gawain did not tremble this time, but shouted at his executioner.

"Strike now, since you have amused yourself too much already with your threats!"

"Now that you have regained your courage, it is time I deal you the death blow."

And having said this, the Green Knight raised the weapon and let it fall onto the knight's bare neck. Amazingly, it did no more than make a slight cut.

Gawain leapt up, seized his lance, and lifted his shield. But the other man threw down his weapon and revealed his true identity. He was Lord Bertilak!

"I promised you a single blow and will not give you more. With the first blow I did not even give you a scratch, since you were sincere and kept faith with the pact we made the first night. The other false blow was because on the second night you also respected my beautiful wife and gave me back her kiss. On the third night you failed me, since the sash you wear was given by my wife and yet you said nothing. For that deception you suffered the third blow. But now I pardon you because you kept the sash not out of malice but for love of life."

From that day on Gawain always carried the green sash with him as a badge of shame—a reminder of the only time he had failed in his loyalty—for loyalty is the mark of a truly chivalrous knight. And as a sign of the high regard they all felt for Gawain, King Arthur's court chose a green sash to be the emblem of the Knights of the Round Table.

THE KNIGHTS OF THE ROUND TABLE

Origin of the Legend

Joseph of Arimathea is often credited with bringing Christianity to Britain. It is said that he brought the Holy Grail containing the blood of Jesus from the Last Supper to Glastonbury, England.

King Arthur is not a historical figure, although his character may have been based on a Briton chieftain who successfully fought the Saxons who were then invading Britain. King Arthur represents the ideal qualities of a medieval king—he is noble, brave, chivalrous, and just. His capital was the legendary Camelot, where he and his knights gathered at the Round Table. The Round Table was significant because it allowed all the knights to be equal, since no one can sit at the head of a round table. Most medieval kingdoms were basedon hierarchies, but Arthur's court was based on fairness and equality.

It has been said that on his death King Arthur was buried beside Guinevere at Glastonbury Abbey, which is believed to be the site of the mythical Avalon.

The Well of the Grail

"We are nearing Avalon!" cried a member of the crew to the boat's master, Joseph of Arimathea, a disciple of Jesus. The boat rocked wildly on churning waves that seemed about to shatter it to pieces.

Joseph caught a glimpse of an island through the mists. He had heard of Britain, that magic land where the Druids knew the powers of the Earth. And for that reason he had decided that it was there he would take the Holy Grail, filled with the blood of Christ, and build the first Christian church. When they had landed, Joseph stuck his staff in the ground and he and his men built a church on that very spot out of clay and willow branches. It was necessary to find a safe hiding place for the Grail, so after some exploration he decided that it should be hidden ina deep well nearby.

"The Grail may only be taken from its hiding place by a warrior who is pure of heart, and ready to bear the message of goodness and light to the world."

Arthur and the Sword

Five centuries later a baby was born who would carry out destiny's grand designs. The baby's father was Uther Pendragon, King of England. Through the enchantment of the wizard Merlin, Uther magically transformed into the duke of Cornwall and produced a baby with the duke's wife, Igraine. In exchange for his magic, Uther gave his baby to Merlin, who named him Arthur and had the knight Sir Ector raise him. At that time, Britain was being attacked by the Saxons. King Uther kept the borders secure until he was poisoned to death. The kingdom then fell into chaos for there was no heir to the throne. Thus the nobles sought out Merlin.

"Oh, wizard," they begged him, "help us choose a new king."

"Wait until Christmas," Merlin told them. "The son of God will find a way to show us who should be king."

When Christmas day arrived, a crowd was gathered in the church to pray for a new king. Among those present was young Arthur. After the prayers, everyone came out of the church and found a solid rock with a sword in it. Seeing in this a sign from heaven, it was decided that whoever could pull the sword from the stone would be the new king.

Hundreds of strong knights attempted without success to pull out the sword. No one noticed young Arthur step forward to try his hand. Arthur took hold of the sword and pulled on it. To his amazement, the sword came free from the rock with ease.

Thus it was decided that Arthur was the one true king of England.

Years later, Arthur broke his sword in battle. Merlin brought the king to an enchantress, the Lady of the Lake. Out of the water, the Lady's hand appeared and held aloft the sword Excalibur (Excalibur means "cut steel"), which Arthur then took. The magical sword ensured that its user would never lose blood in battle.

Camelot and the Knights of the Round Table

In spite of the disapproval of many who were opposed to such a young man taking power, Arthur gathered the bravest knights around him in the castle of Camelot. The country enjoyed twelve years of peace and prosperity, so the king was respected by his subjects and feared by his enemies. He asked for the hand of Princess Guinevere of Cameliard. Guinevere's father sent Uther Pendragon's round table as a wedding gift.

The Round Table ensured that all the knights would be treated as equals. Each knight swore an oath of fellowship to King Arthur, England, and each other.

During a meeting about different matters of concern to the court, a peal of thunder was heard in the hall and then a lightning bolt struck the center of the table, showing the golden image of the Grail. Sir Gawain was the first to rise and speak to his companions: "As the existence of the Holy Grail has been revealed to us, tomorrow I will set out in search of it and will not return to Camelot until we have it with us, to bring light, goodness, and wisdom to this land."

Bors, Lancelot and his son Galahad, Parzival, and many other distinguished knights—along with Arthur himself—joined Gawain, and on these quests they met with perilous adventures that obliged them to fight against goblins and dragons. The Grail quest brought death to many knights, which weakened the court and encouraged those who plotted to take power.

In their last adventure, Galahad, Parzival, and Bors came to the mystical city of Sarras, where the Grail was being kept. They failed to locate the Grail, and the local king was afraid of the knights so he locked them up in a dungeon for a year. During all that time the Grail miraculously provided them with food and drink. However, only Sir Bors made it back to Camelot.

Betrayals in Camelot

When Arthur learned that his beloved wife, Guinevere, was in love with one of his favorite knights, Sir Lancelot, the saddened and enraged king condemned her to burn at the stake.

The King's best knights guarded the queen, yet Lancelot freed her, and together they fled to France.

"Let all the knights follow me to avenge this double treason!" King Arthur ordered, wild with anger.

While they pursued the lovers without success, the court of Camelot was left in the custody of the king's son, Mordred. Mordred's mother was not married to Arthur, so he had no legal claim to the throne. But on their return, Arthur and his knights found that Mordred had usurped the throne, crowning himself the king of England.

"Let weapons speak and mete out justice." Arthur declared.

These words unleashed a terrible battle between the two forces. Many brave knights were killed, including Sir Gawain. In a merciless fight, Arthur killed his son with his lance after having been mortally wounded himself.

Before taking his last breath, Arthur called Sir Bedivere, one of his most faithful knights, and asked him to throw the sword Excalibur into the water. The knight resolved to do so and at once the bare arm of the Lady of the Lake caught the sword and took it down into the depths forever.

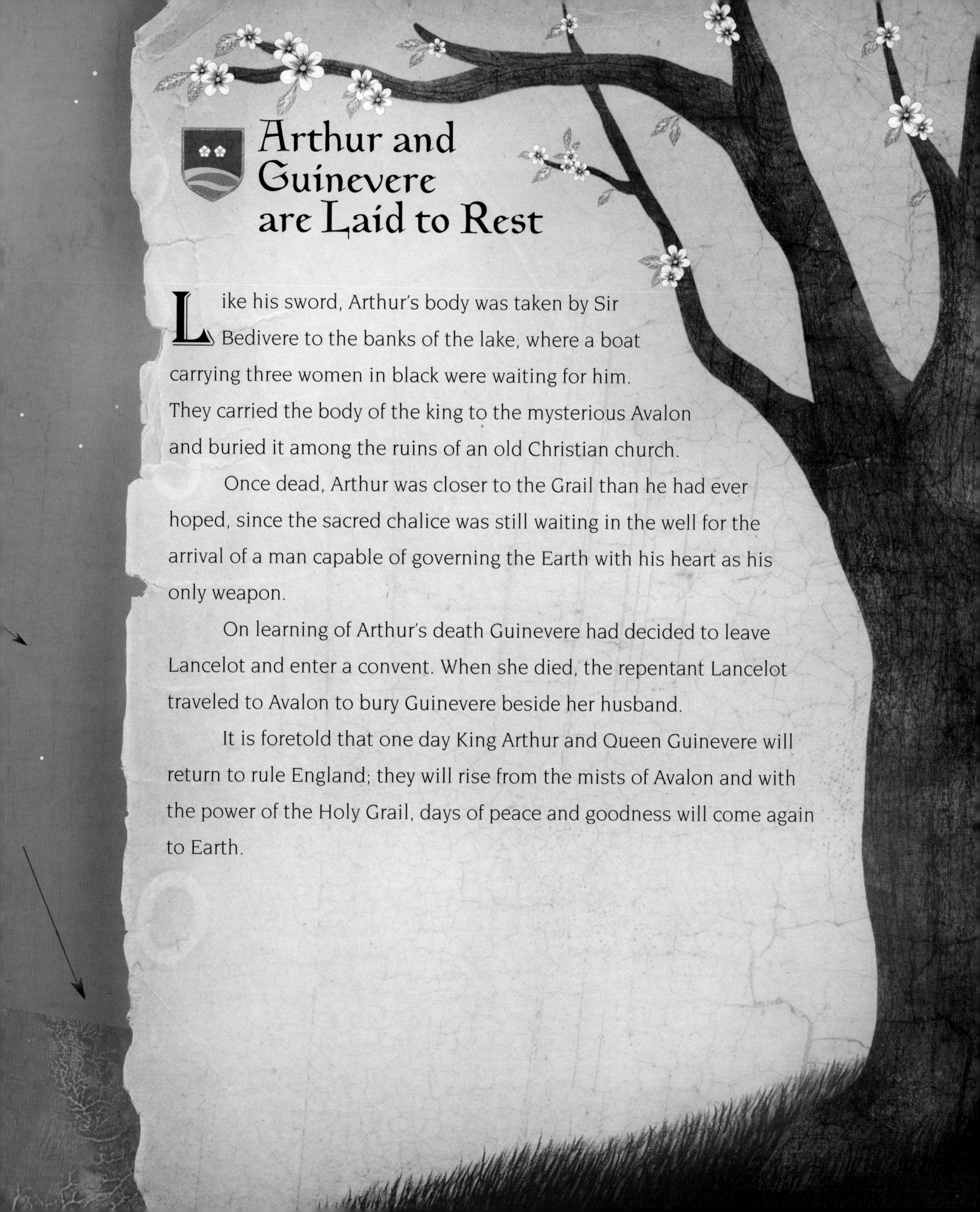

Arthur and Guinevere are Laid to Rest

Like his sword, Arthur's body was taken by Sir Bedivere to the banks of the lake, where a boat carrying three women in black were waiting for him. They carried the body of the king to the mysterious Avalon and buried it among the ruins of an old Christian church.

Once dead, Arthur was closer to the Grail than he had ever hoped, since the sacred chalice was still waiting in the well for the arrival of a man capable of governing the Earth with his heart as his only weapon.

On learning of Arthur's death Guinevere had decided to leave Lancelot and enter a convent. When she died, the repentant Lancelot traveled to Avalon to bury Guinevere beside her husband.

It is foretold that one day King Arthur and Queen Guinevere will return to rule England; they will rise from the mists of Avalon and with the power of the Holy Grail, days of peace and goodness will come again to Earth.

THE SONG OF THE NIBELUNGS

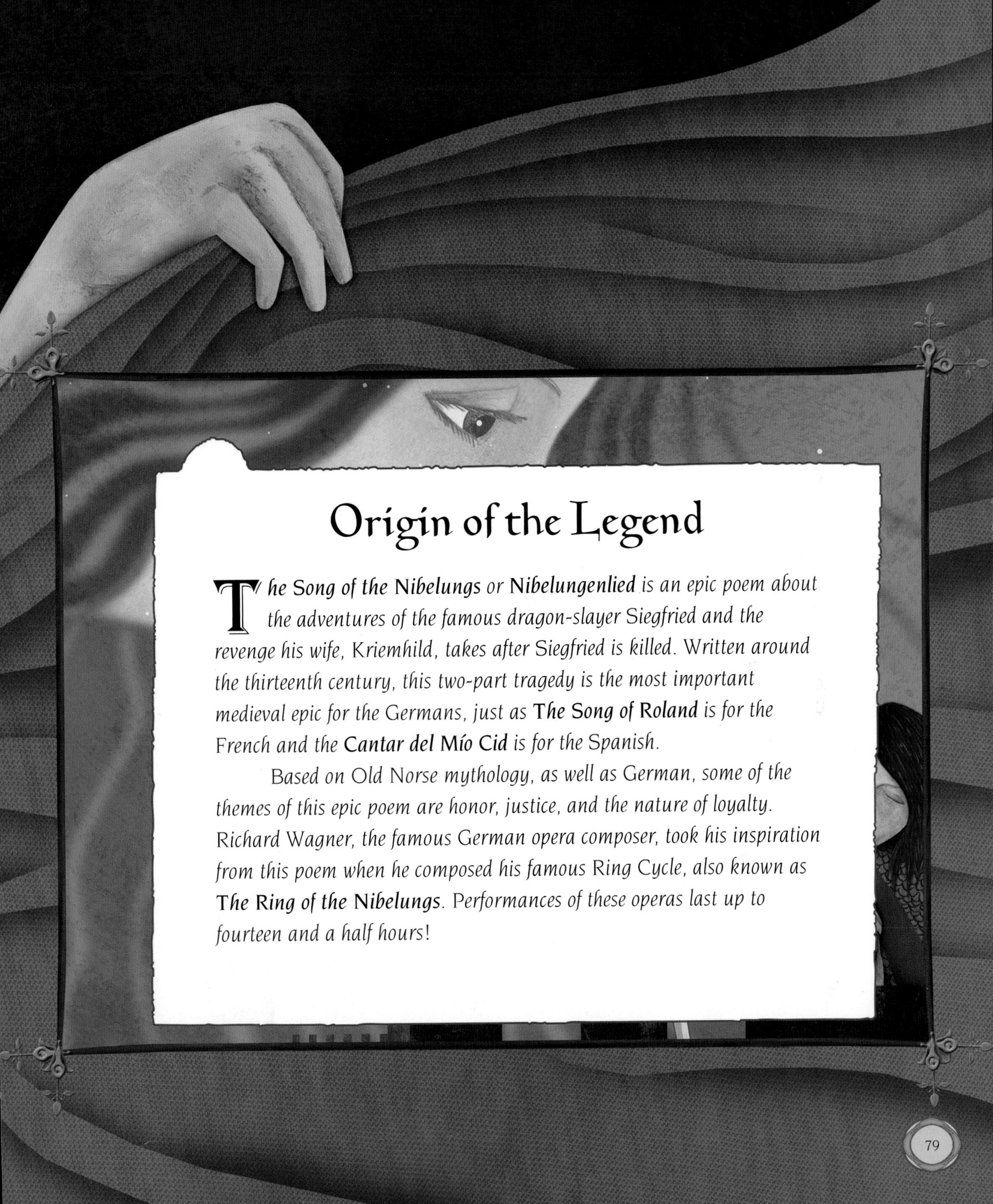

Origin of the Legend

*The **Song of the Nibelungs** or **Nibelungenlied** is an epic poem about the adventures of the famous dragon-slayer Siegfried and the revenge his wife, Kriemhild, takes after Siegfried is killed. Written around the thirteenth century, this two-part tragedy is the most important medieval epic for the Germans, just as **The Song of Roland** is for the French and the **Cantar del Mío Cid** is for the Spanish.*

*Based on Old Norse mythology, as well as German, some of the themes of this epic poem are honor, justice, and the nature of loyalty. Richard Wagner, the famous German opera composer, took his inspiration from this poem when he composed his famous Ring Cycle, also known as **The Ring of the Nibelungs**. Performances of these operas last up to fourteen and a half hours!*

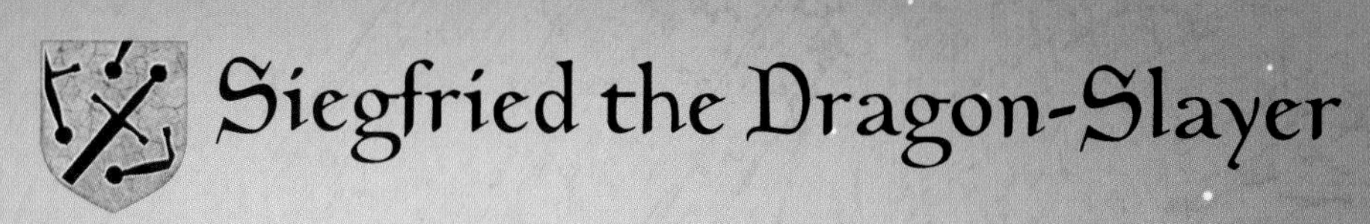

Siegfried the Dragon-Slayer

Siegfried was the son of a noble king of the Netherlands, and in his time there was no warrior more courageous. He was known far and wide for having defeated the powerful king of the Nibelungs and his two sons. Thus he had won their treasure, as well as a magical cloak from a dwarf who had tried to steal the treasure from Siegfried.

The young Siegfried was also famous for having vanquished a dragon with his own hands. After bathing in the dragon's blood, his skin had become invulnerable—no weapon could pierce it—except for a small place on Siegfried's back where a linden leaf had fallen while he was bathing. The dragon's blood had not covered that tiny spot.

Shortly after he was dubbed a knight, the valiant Siegfried heard it said that in the court of Burgundy there lived a princess named Kriemhild whose beauty and nobility were so remarkable that all who knew her considered her to be the lady most worthy of being loved.

Siegfried decided that he had to have Kriemhild for his wife. With this idea he set off for Burgundy and was received with great honor at the court of King Gunther, Kriemhild's brother. For more than a year he lived at Gunther's court, enjoying the hospitality of the king, without seeing Kriemhild. When they finally met, young Siegfried and Kriemhild fell deeply in love.

The Conquest of Queen Brünhild

Far away, in the remote land of Iceland, there lived a queen called Brünhild. She was famous for her beauty, as well as for her strength. Whoever aspired to win her love had to pass three tests, and if he failed just one of them he would lose his head.

King Gunther was ready to take the risk to win the lady's love, and he begged Siegfried to accompany him on the journey and help him.

"If you allow your sister to be my wife," Siegfried replied, "I am prepared to do it."

"If I return to this country with Queen Brünhild," the king said, "I will give you my sister in marriage."

After making this agreement, the two friends left for Iceland. Siegfried carried with him his magic cape, which had the power to make him invisible and gave him the strength of twelve men. Siegfried pretended to be a vassal of King Gunther's.

It was only thanks to Siegfried and his cape that Gunther was able to pass those difficult tests. At one point Gunther had to throw a lance so heavy that three men could scarcely lift it, and it was Siegfried's invisible hand that actually threw it while the king only made a gesture.

So Brünhild believed that Gunther had passed those tests that all other men had found impossible and she set off with him to his kingdom to become his wife.

The Wedding Night

Everyone at court was very happy about the celebration of that double wedding—everyone except Brünhild.

"I cannot understand why you are giving your sister to Siegfried, when he is only your vassal," she said, full of suspicion and distrust.

On the wedding night, Brünhild used her strength, which was truly supernatural, to resist her husband. After she had beaten him, she tied him up and left him hanging from a nail in the wall all night. The king was humiliated, and Siegfried was very upset when, the next day, he found out what had happened. So he proposed to help Gunther.

On the second night after the wedding he followed the couple to their bedroom wrapped in his magic cloak. When the torches were put out he engaged in a fierce combat with Brünhild until he made her submit. The exploit almost cost him his life, since the queen's strength was so extraordinary.

Siegfried took from Brünhild a ring and a lovely sash without her realizing it. The queen surrendered to her husband's love and from then on lost her strength forever.

The Hatred Between the Two Queens

Siegfried and Kriemhild left for the kingdom of the Netherlands. Years passed and Brünhild continued to wonder why Siegfried did not pay homage and fealty to his lord, King Gunther. The couple was invited to Gunther's court for a tournament, and when the two ladies were sitting together they began to argue about which of their husbands was the nobler of the two.

"When Gunther came to Iceland to conquer my love," Brünhild said, "Siegfried himself said he was the king's vassal."

Kriemhild was furious, because she knew the truth about the conquest of Brünhild and thought that both those kingdoms should belong by rights to her husband. Blinded by anger, she thoughtlessly showed Brünhild the ring and the sash that Siegfried had taken from her on the wedding night and revealed that he had been the one who actually conquered her.

Brünhild went crying to Gunther and begged him to avenge that insult. The king then demanded that Siegfried swear that he had never abused the queen's virtue and never bragged of having done so. When Siegfried expressed his readiness to take the oath, the king knew that he was innocent and that the person guilty of offending Brünhild had been his sister.

From that moment on the two queens became terrible enemies.

The Betrayal

Many of the knights of the court were unhappy to see the lady Brünhild so tormented. The cruel Hagen, one of King Gunther's vassals, approached her one day to learn the reason for her tears. The queen told him what had happened and said she could never be happy again unless Siegfried was made to pay for his insult.

Then Hagen, together with some other knights, made a plan to murder Siegfried. They even convinced Gunther that Siegfried must die by telling him that if Siegfried lived he would end up conquering a great part of Gunther's kingdom.

Hagen knew that when Siegfried had bathed in the dragon's blood a linden leaf had fallen and covered part of his body, but he didn't know where it had fallen, so he devised a plot to trick Siegfried and Kriemhild.

The plotters cleverly planted signs of an imminent invasion by the Saxons and the Danes. With that excuse, Hagen asked Kriemhild to indicate what part of Siegfried's body was vulnerable so that he could protect him in battle. The naïve Kriemhild told him that it was on the hero's back, between his shoulder blades, and even agreed to sew a cross on the exact spot, thinking that in this way she would be protecting her husband. Little did she know she was only helping in Siegfried's murder.

The Death of Siegfried

Hagen and Gunther then planned a hunt in the forest and went out together with Siegfried and some other knights.

That day the hero displayed every bit of his valor, hunting down all alone a bear, a lion, a wild boar, and many other beasts.

When at nightfall the men sat down to eat and refresh themselves, hungry and thirsty, it was discovered that Hagen had forgotten the wine. Slyly, Hagen told Siegfried that nearby there was a spring and challenged him to a race there, carrying their lances.

Siegfried was of course the first to reach the spring. He lay down his weapon and knelt to drink. It was then that Hagen drove his lance with all his strength into the place where Kriemhild had sewn the mark. The hero's blood dyed the flowers red.

Many knights and ladies wept over the death of the brave and noble Siegfried, but no one so much as his wife.

Kriemheld knew at once who the guilty parties were and swore she would not die until she had avenged the cruel and cowardly murder. She spent years in mourning, weeping over the loss of her beloved husband. Then she married the powerful King Etzel of the Huns and began to plot the perfect revenge—Hagen and Gunther would pay for their deeds!

Kriemheld invited Hagen and Gunther and the other Burgundians to Etzel, but instead of welcoming them, a great slaughter ensued and the two powerful Germanic tribes were wiped out in a fearsome battle.

ROBIN HOOD

Origin of the Legend

In thirteenth century England, minstrels sang of the exploits of Robin Hood. His name came from the red hood he wore. He was a generous hero who defended the oppressed. To do so he stole from the rich to distribute the goods among the poor.

According to the legend, Robin Hood hid himself deep in Sherwood Forest, near Nottingham, where the villainous Sheriff was in charge of collecting the abusive taxes that Prince John exacted from the subjects of his brother, Richard the Lionheart. Prince John had taken the throne of his brother while Richard was off fighting in the Crusades.

Written mentions of Robin Hood have appeared since the late fourteenth century, but it wasn't until the beginning of the sixteenth century that many ballads were printed about his adventures. It is during this period that a romantic association with Maid Marian, a girl belonging to the nobility, first appeared. Countless adaptations of this legend have come down to us, in the form of songs, novels, plays, and films.

The Bandit

Deep in Sherwood Forest, not far from the English town of Nottingham, lived a famous outlaw who hated injustice. For that reason he robbed the rich and gave the money to the poor. He fought unfairness and tyranny. The people loved him and knew him by the name of Robin Hood.

Norman invaders had recently conquered England, robbing the Saxon people and taking the best lands, while they subjected the Saxons to a life of cruelty. But they had not been able to get rid of Robin Hood. No one was capable of catching the popular bandit, neither the corrupt Sheriff of Nottingham nor Prince John—who had taken over the throne of England from his brother, King Richard the Lionheart, while he was away fighting in the Crusades.

With Robin there lived a group of his faithful followers, men whose homes and lands had been taken from them. They were known as Robin's Merry Men and had joined together to combat the Norman soldiers and the merciless sheriff, who demanded huge taxes from the poor, forcing them to live in misery.

England's Best Archer

Among his friends and followers was Will Scarlett, a renowned archer. But Robin himself was famous for being the best archer in all of England.

One night Robin and his band were hiding in a clearing in the woods eating meat they had stolen from the herds of the prince's sheriff.

"You take too many risks, Robin," said his friend Little John (who was actually quite big). "The next time we do a robbery like this one they'll put our heads in a noose."

"Nonsense. Robbery? What robbery? We've just taken what we needed."

Suddenly a young man arrived, coming from the town. He brought with him a piece of parchment that he was eager to show Robin.

"Well, well," Robin said when he had read it. "It seems our dear friend, the sheriff, is looking for a bit of fun. He is organizing a competition at the castle to find the best archer in England. The prize for the winner will be a silver arrow."

"Robin, dear," interjected Marian, his bride-to-be, "surely you're not thinking of going. Don't you see it's a trap?"

"Marian is quite right," said Friar Tuck, another one of the members of the band. "He knows you're the best archer in England."

"And he also knows you won't be able to resist the challenge," Will added.

"Of course it's a trap," Robin said. "I know that as well as you do. But that is all the more reason to accept the challenge and beat the sheriff at his own game. Listen to me carefully; we shall prepare a plan."

The Contest

A week later a great crowd gathered in the courtyard of the castle. Prince John, the sheriff, and their guards were together on a high platform overlooking the people.

"I trust our men are fully prepared to catch Robin Hood," the Sheriff of Nottingham said.

"Of course, milord. It will be a memorable day," answered one of his guards.

The sheriff announced the rules of the competition while he scanned the crowd of contestants in search of anyone who looked suspicious. Robin had never allowed himself to be seen, so the sheriff did not know what he looked like. He did, however, observe a young man in a green hood, who seemed to be a likely suspect.

Finally, at the sound of a trumpet, the contest began.

As the trials became more difficult, more and more contestants were eliminated. Soon there were only five left. Two were Norman soldiers and the other three were Saxons. There was one among them who was clearly the best archer. This was the mysterious hooded man, whose arrow always went straight to the bull's eye.

IIIII Arrest That Man!

When the contest went into its final phase and it was time for the man in the green hood to take his turn, the Norman guards were close by, ready to act.

All the spectators held their breath when the skillful archer drew his bow. His arrow, as always, went straight to the exact center of the target. It was without doubt the best shot of the day.

The Saxons joyfully celebrated the victory, but suddenly mayhem ensued.

"Arrest that man!" shouted the enraged sheriff.

The soldiers obeyed his orders, and the Sheriff of Nottingham spoke to the man in the hood.

"So we meet at last, Robin Hood," he said smugly. "Have you anything to say to me before I send you to the gallows?"

"Only that I am not the person for whom you are looking," the young man replied.

"Hah! And I am not the Sheriff of Nottingham. Guards, take him away!" he ordered, burning with the desire for revenge.

"One moment, sir," said one of the Norman soldiers. "This man is telling the truth. He is not Robin Hood."

"How do you know that?" shouted the sheriff.

"His name is Will Scarlett. And I am Robin Hood," the soldier said, taking off his helmet. "And it is time to finish this! Now!"

Before anyone could react, another one of the men who was supposed to be a soldier took out a dagger and

threatened the sheriff with it. Nottingham's men had no idea what to do to defend him.

"Help me, you idiots!" he shouted in desperation.

"One false move and we will cut his throat," Robin Hood warned. "You had better put down your weapons. And if you need any more reason to do as I say, just look around you."

Last Arrow

The Norman soldiers turned and saw more and more outlaws from Robin Hood's band stepping forth from among the crowd.

"The sheriff wanted to trap me, but we have managed to ruin the day for him," laughed Robin Hood.

The crowd seemed happy with the outcome, and the Sheriff of Nottingham tried one last trick to try to make Robin Hood look foolish.

"Nonetheless, Robin," he said, "it seems you have not proved yourself to be the best archer, since this friend of yours has shown more talent."

"Do you mind if I give a little demonstration?" Robin asked his friend.

"Go right ahead, Robin," Will answered courteously.

Robin Hood drew his bow and aimed for the target where his friend's arrow was still firmly planted in the center.

The arrow flew with the greatest precision and, to the amazement of all, split Will's arrow in two and struck the center of the target. Even the Norman soldiers were impressed.

The people applauded their hero and looked forward to his next feat, for they knew they had not seen the last of Robin Hood!

Back in the Woods

"Well, it seems I have won the silver arrow," Robin exclaimed with a laugh.

He went to get it, and at that moment Marian arrived, leading four horses.

"Shall we go home, Robin?" she said.

"Of course, Marian," he answered. "And it seems to me that we should take our friend the sheriff with us. It's a beautiful day and he will enjoy the ride."

Will lifted the sheriff onto one of the horses and tied his hands to the saddle. Robin, with Marian at his side, galloped off in the direction of Sherwood Forest.

They say the sheriff appeared hours later, naked and tied to the horse, so that the people could laugh at him.

Robin's fight against the Normans did not end here, and his band of Merry Men met with many more adventures. The fame of this charming bandit spread throughout England, and many of the poor still remember him when they fight against tyranny.

THE SONG OF MY CID

Origin of the Legend

The **Song of My Cid** *or* **El Cantar del Mío Cid**, *is a Spanish epic poem written in the twelfth century. Some believe that a man named Per Abbat was the author, but it is more likely that he merely copied down the poem from an earlier source. His handwritten copy is preserved at the National Library of Spain, and dates to the year 1207. The story is based on a real person, a Castilian knight named Rodrigo Díaz de Vivar, also known as Cid Campeador, Lord Conqueror. He became a Spanish national hero for unifying Spain.* **The Song of My Cid** *tells of El Cid's banishment from the kingdom of Castile, his conquering of Valencia, and his eventual reunion with King Alfonso VI of Castile.*

The Song of My Cid *is the first and oldest* **cantar de gesta**, *or song of deeds, in Spanish literature. Unlike most medieval epics, the story does not include any magical elements. Its theme is the triumph of true nobility over false nobility.*

The Exile of El Cid

Rodrigo Díaz de Vivar was a noble knight in the service of King Alfonso of Castile. All his vassals loved him and called him *Mío Cid*, which means something like "my lord" since they well knew of his courage on the battlefield. They also called him the *Campeador*, meaning the "champion" or the "conqueror."

But the nobility of El Cid aroused the envy of Count Ordóñez, who the Campeador had also beaten in a fight. For that reason the count felt humiliated, so he accused El Cid before the king of having kept for himself part of the taxes he had been in charge of collecting for the monarch.

King Alfonso believed this slander and exiled El Cid from Castile, stripping him of all his property. His vassals, however, did not wish to abandon him. El Cid left his palace in the town of Vivar, near the city of Burgos, accompanied by sixty faithful men.

It was with great sadness that El Cid took leave of his wife, Jimena, and his two daughters, Elvira and Sol, putting them in the care of the abbot of the monastery of San Pedro de Cardeña, for as long as his exile might last.

The Conquests of El Cid

El Cid and his faithful men left their land and ventured into territory that had once belonged to Christian Spain, but was now governed by Muslim kings. They were determined to conquer them anew, and other men joined to support them in their endeavor.

On reaching the gates of Alcocer, they surrounded and laid siege to the castle for fifteen weeks and finally succeeded in conquering it. When they raised their flags high on the battlements, the conquered people hurried to ask the aid of the king of Valencia, Tamin. The king sent an army of three thousand men to fight El Cid, who had only six hundred fighters.

Tamin's men surrounded the castle and left El Cid's army without food or water. But after four weeks of resistance, El Cid and his men met Tamin's forces on the field of battle and succeeded in defeating them.

El Cid sent King Alfonso the best part of the enormous amount of plunder they had taken. Even then the monarch would not pardon him, though he allowed the knights who wished to go and fight with him.

With his army reinforced, El Cid continued winning back Christian lands for years—Saragossa, Huesca, Teruel—all fell before him. Nothing and no one could resist his advance.

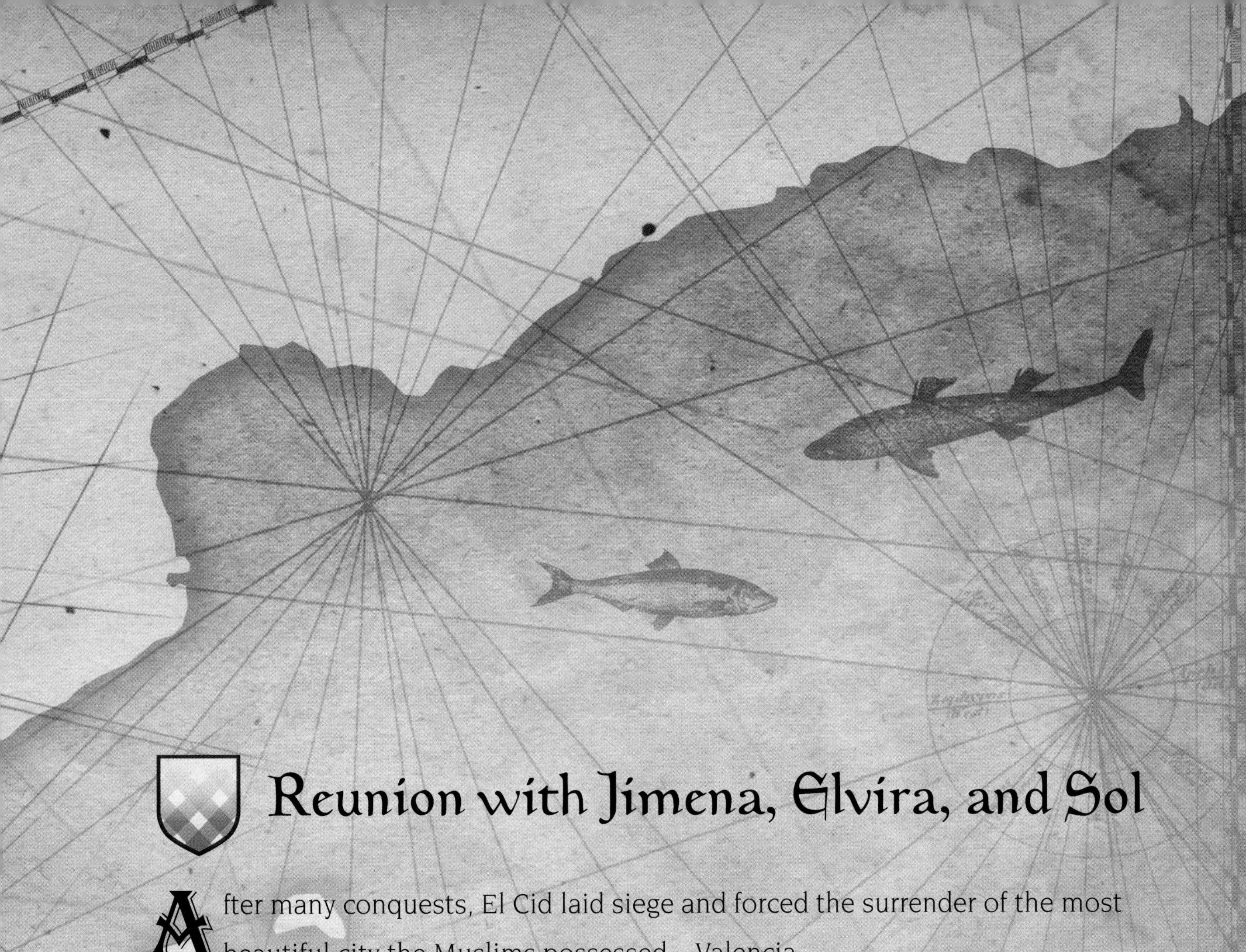

Reunion with Jimena, Elvira, and Sol

After many conquests, El Cid laid siege and forced the surrender of the most beautiful city the Muslims possessed—Valencia.

The richness of the plunder was incalculable, and El Cid sent one of his most faithful knights to deliver a part to King Alfonso and to beg him, at the same time, to permit his wife and daughters to rejoin him in the land of Valencia.

When the king received El Cid's gifts, two ambitious young men, Fernando and Diego, happened to be with him. They were the *infantes*, or princes, of Carrión. Hearing of El Cid's wealth stirred their greed, and they thought it would be an excellent piece of business to marry his daughters, Elvira and Sol.

The king permitted Jimena and her daughters to be reunited with El Cid in Valencia. Mounted on his famous horse, Babieca, El Cid went out to welcome them at the gates of the city, and the family could not have been happier when they met again, since they had suffered the pain of separation for five long years.

The King's Pardon

When the Christians were happily installed in Valencia, having taken possession of houses and lands, the king of Morocco, Yusef, sailed with a fleet of fifty thousand soldiers to regain the city.

Nonetheless El Cid, in the most famous of all the battles he fought, succeeded in defeating them with only four thousand men. He himself fought hand to hand against King Yusef and took him prisoner.

This battle increased El Cid's renown and his wealth, and once again he sent part of the plunder of battle to the king as a sign of his fealty and obedience.

And once again the *infantes* of Carrión happened to be in the presence of the king when this occurred, and Fernando and Diego begged him to ask the Campeador to let them take his daughters for their wives.

The king's heart was softened by El Cid's loyalty and sent him a message saying that he wished to meet with him in the court at Toledo. Unfortunately, he also yielded to the desires of the two ambitious young men, and asked for the hands of El Cid's two daughters for the *infantes* of Carrión.

El Cid felt great joy on meeting once again with his king, who opened his heart to him and returned all his honors. Nonetheless, during the fifteen days of celebrations for the weddings of his daughters he went about with a bowed head, because the *infantes'* request had aroused his distrust and suspicion, and he had only agreed to give his daughters to them because he could not refuse his king.

The Outrage of the Infantes

For two years the *infantes* lived in wealth and comfort in Valencia, receiving every attention from El Cid and his family. But among the Campeador's men their reputation as cowards grew day by day, though out of goodwill the men kept their opinions a secret from their lord.

On one occasion a lion that had been caged up in the cellars of the palace escaped, and the two princes behaved in such a cowardly fashion that from then on they were continually laughed at. Deeply humiliated, they began to plan their revenge.

Fernando and Diego asked El Cid to allow them to return to Castile with his daughters to show them their possessions. El Cid, unsuspecting, agreed to the journey. Félez Muñoz, the Campeador's nephew, accompanied the *infantes* and their wives.

Once they were in the land of Castile, the company rode into a forest and camped there for the night. But before dawn the two terrible princes fell upon their wives and, after stripping off their clothes, they tied them to a tree trunk and whipped them mercilessly.

Those cowardly men, in their madness, were trying to free themselves of the sense of humiliation they felt, since they were ashamed of being such spineless creatures.

The wicked princes fled, leaving their wives for dead, but Félez Muñoz saved them and hurriedly returned to Valencia in search of El Cid.

The Vengeance of El Mio Cid

El Mío Cid wept long and bitterly with his daughters when he saw them and learned of how they had been insulted. With a terrible bitterness in his heart he asked King Alfonso to force the *infantes* to pay for their evil deed.

The king heard El Cid's demands and summoned the court of Toledo.

"What do you ask of the guilty parties?" the king asked him.

"I ask to challenge the two cowards," he declared.

Two of his most loyal knights, Pedro Bermúdez and Martín Antolínez, stepped forward to stop him. They were unwilling to allow the noble El Cid to lower himself by fighting with such scoundrels and offered to fight in his place.

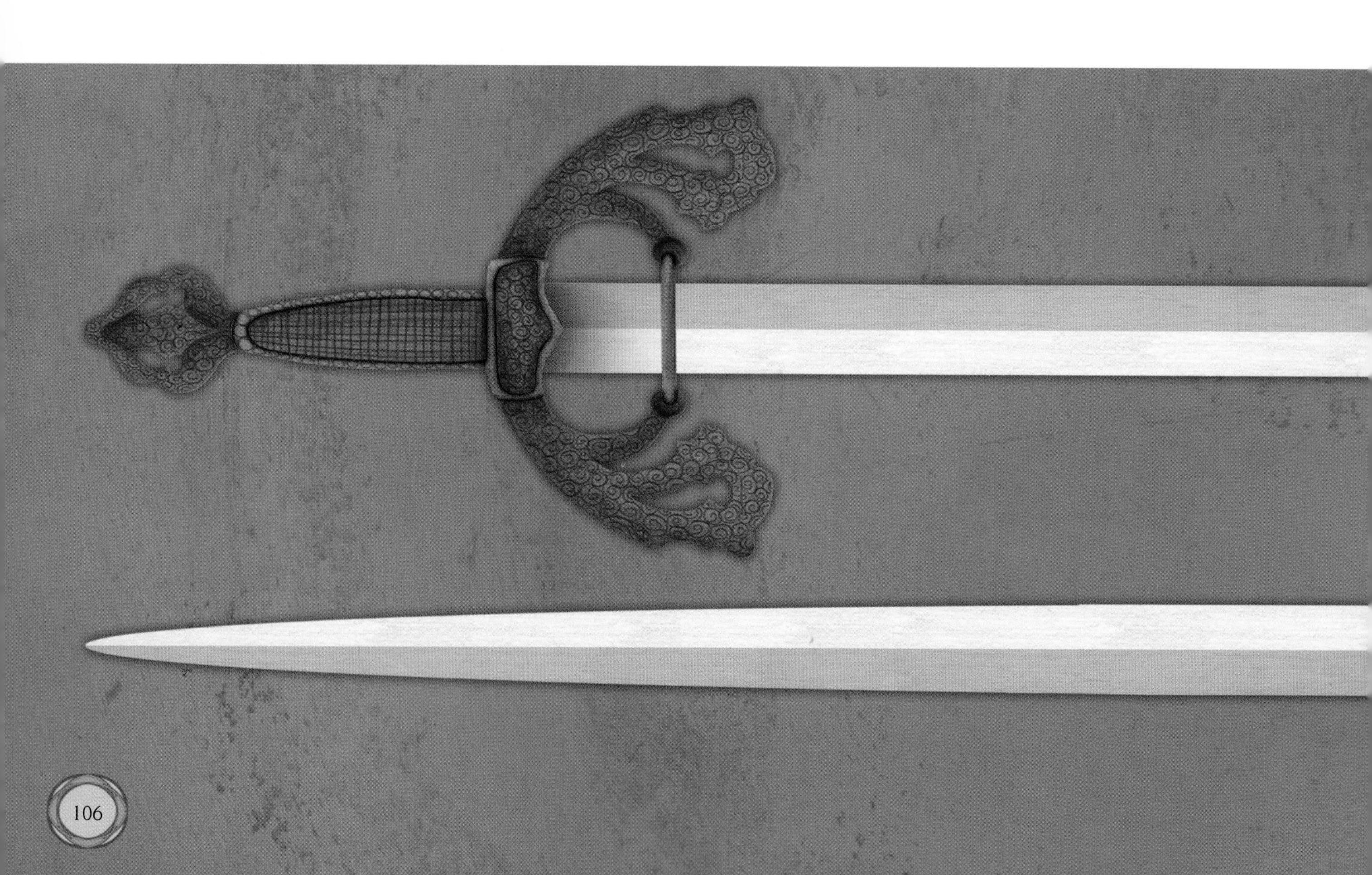

Three weeks later the combat took place and the two princes, like the cowards they were, trembled to see Tizona and Colada, El Cid's two finest swords, raised against them.

Very soon Prince Fernando yielded to Pedro Bermúdez, when Pedro, with his first blow, knocked him off his horse. His brother Diego did the same, fleeing in terror when Antolínez split open his helmet and shattered his armor with a single blow.

The honor of El Cid and his daughters was thus restored, and the kings of Navarre and Aragon asked Elvira and Sol to marry their sons. This news was received with great joy in all the court, since the ladies would thus become queens of Aragon and Navarre and El Cid and his family would finally receive the happiness and honors they so richly deserved.

Heroes, Heroines, and Villains

Lancelot
(the Knight of the Cart)

Parzival

Roland

Romeo and Juliet

Yvain
(the Knight of the Lion)

Tristan and Isolde

Sir Gawain

King Arthur

Queen Guinevere

Robin Hood

Will Scarlett

Sheriff of
Nottingham

Siegfried

Queen Kriemhild
and Queen Brünhild

El Cid
(Rodrigo Díaz de Vivar)

Celebrated Castles, Scenes, and Settings

Lancelot's
"Kingdom of No Return"
(King Bademagu's castle)

Snow-capped mountains
on Parzival's quest

Roncesvalles,
where Roland gave battle

Romeo and Juliet's
city of Verona

Yvain's
magical fountain

Isolde's
castle in Cornwall

Gawain's
Green Chapel

King Arthur's
Camelot

Castle of
the Nibelungs

Robin Hood's
Sherwood Forest

El Cid's
castle in Valencia

To the Noble
Reader: Retell the
marvelous exploits and
adventures portrayed within
these pages and become a
celebrated modern-day
minstrel!